Ben Bones
&
The Twin Pistols

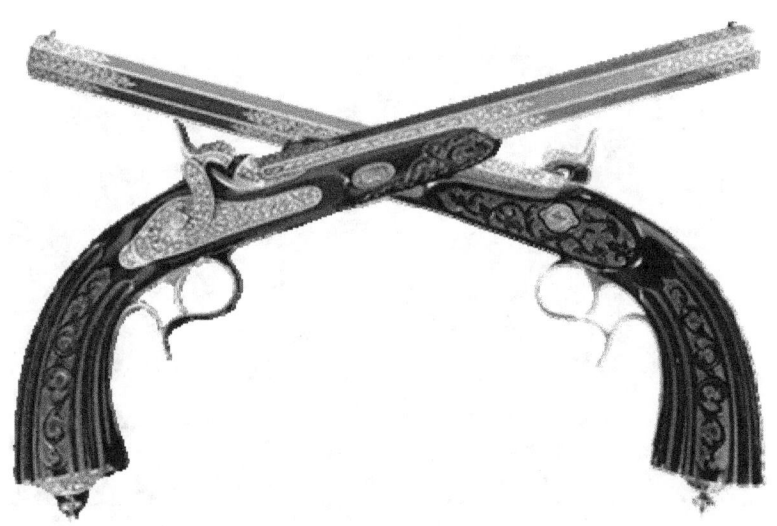

A Ben Bones Genealogical Misadventure

Michael F. Havelin

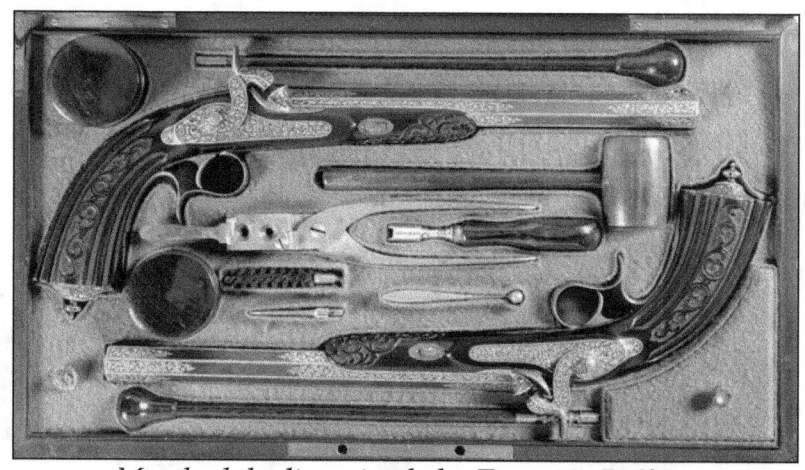

Matched dueling pistols by François Prélat.

Dedication

This book is dedicated, with the greatest respect, to the literate people of the world. May there be ever more of us.

A Few Words About This Book

Oct, 2017   I started this book with a vague idea to write about a pair of dueling pistols that was split by inheritance to twin brothers. Why did I have this idea? Who knows? But I recognized it as the kernel of a story. I started cogitatin' on it.

Before I knew it, I had characters, the weapons, several duels, and another Ben Bones adventure percolating.

Initially, the book was planned to be bifurcated: a "Past" section to establish the historical basis, and a "Present" part where all the Ben Bones action happens.

My WNCMysterians.org fellow and sister writers accused me of writing "term papers" (info dumps) on all the technical and historical material. They were right, so I went back and completely reorganized the book.

Every book is its own experiment, but this Past/Present experiment didn't work as I thought it would. I looked back at the earlier Ben Bones misadventures and then returned to the original formula of tracking the story over the course of a week or so of Bones' researches. These are novels of limited time frame. It's a system that works and is simple to take care of.

It has taken almost a year for the plot to coalesce, but the writing went well.

Note: Although I do extensive research for the Ben Bones series of genealogical misadventures, some of the dates and other facts are tweaked to fit my story. The basic facts are mostly correct.

Acknowledgements

- Fellow Mensan Lori Gutzmann, who re-fired my genealogical flame and set me once again on Ben Bones' adventurous road.
- Blake Terry, Wilson & Terry Auction Company in Weaverville, NC (wilsonandteryyauction.net).
- Lauren Brunk – Brunk Auctions, Asheville, NC (brunkauctions.com).
- Parker Kennedy, long-time friend and fellow musical co-conspirator in *The Bougalieu*, and the owner of *Caffé Luna*, a fine Italian restaurant located at 136 East Hargett St., Downtown Raleigh, North Carolina (919) 832-6090), for allowing me to use his place as a scene in this Ben Bones misadventure. Hey, Parker, it's free advertising.
- Meredith Lenell, a friend of years with keen and practical insights.
- The Internet, which enabled research at distance.
- The Havelin Family Poets: Fred, James, Kate, and myself. All of us seem to share the same genetic defect: a tendency to authorship.
- And most important, the WNC Mysterians Writers' Critique Group of Asheville, North Carolina (WNCMysterians.org), who kept me on the unmapped road to completion and seeming literary competence.

Contemporary Characters

- **Benjamin S. Bones** – Consulting Genealogist and self-proclaimed "Articulator of Family Skeletons." Our protagonist.
- **Wallace Davidi Arrington, Esq.** – Raleigh attorney and gun collector. Married a direct lineal descendant of Alfonso Davidi (Alfred Davisson in America) and added the Davidi name to his own. Third great-grandson (by marriage) of Alfred Davis. Owner by inheritance of one of the Prélat dueling pistols. His goal is to reunite the Prélat pistol set.
- **Celine Davisson Benton Arrington** – Wallace Arrington's harpy wife.
- **Fiona Arley Arrington** – Daughter of Celine and Wallace Arrington. Thespian and lesbian.
- **Victor Davidi Arrington** – Celine and Wallace Arrington's petty criminal son.
- **Simmy Whittington** – Housekeeper at Wallace Arrington's home in Raleigh. Has been with the family a long time.
- **Carla Davis Amalfi** – Wallace Arrington's contemporary in the present and a direct lineal descendant of Alfred Davis. Arrington's fourth cousin by marriage. Does she still have the other pistol? What's her agenda?
- **Odile Obregon** – Owner/auctioneer at Obregon-Meller Auctions, a Raleigh auction house.
- **Detective Emiliano Perez** – Detective who "catches" the Arrington shooting at Obregon-Meller Auctions.
- **Portella Elnora Bakkernon DeNight** – Genealogist who's done genealogical research for Arrington, Esq.
- **Zig** – Wallace Arrington's driver and bodyguard. Ex-military. Doesn't say much but knows his business.
- **Guilt & Innocence** – Wallace Arrington's matched pair of Dobermans.

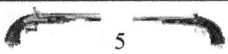

Characters of Historical Interest

- **François Prélat** – Parisian gunsmith who, in 1838, made the set of dueling pistols that are at the heart of this story.
- **Lieutenant Romano** – Well-known braggart and duelist who killed Stefano Davidi. He was subsequently killed by Stefano's brother Alfonso in Salerno, Italy in 1838 in the first duel with the Prélat pistol set.
- **Bellitro** – Lieutenant Romano's second, killed by Alfonso Davidi in Salerno, Italy in 1838.
- **Stefano Davidi** – Younger brother of Alfonso. Killed in a sword duel in Salerno, Italy in 1838 by Lieutenant Romano.
- **Alfonso Davidi** – Older brother of Stefano. Revenged his younger brother's death by killing two men with the Prélat pistols he purchased in Paris specifically for the purpose. Migrated to England after the duels, changed name to Alfred Davis, and, a trained chemist, he built the Davis Match Works business.
- **Carlo Davidi (Charles Davis)** – First-born of the Alfonso's twins. Following the tradition of primogeniture, he was the inheritor of Davis Match and half of the Prélat gun set.
- **Armond Davidi (Armond Davis)** – Second-born by minutes of Alfonso's twins. Left England after being largely cut out of Alfred's will via primogeniture. He arrived in America destitute, changed his name to Armond Davisson, and prospered.

Table of Contents

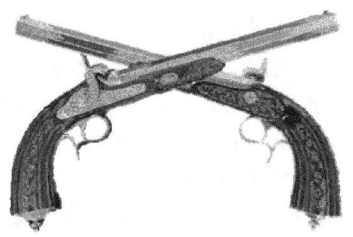

1838, Salerno, Italy

The Clang of Steel

The morning air was cool. A light breeze blew intermittently. The scent of flowers thrilled Salerno residents' nostrils. But there was danger in the air as well, perhaps even death. It took the form of a challenge.

"I am pleased to invite you to a meeting to settle certain matters that rankle between our principals." Having delivered his authorized message from Lieutenant Romano, Mario Bellitro stood at attention awaiting the expected answer. There could be only one: acceptance of the proffered challenge. Anything less would brand Stefano a coward. The Davidi family honor was at stake.

Stefano Davidi thought for only a minute before responding. His answer was predetermined, unavoidable, inevitable. Nonetheless, he still had to be careful in how he expressed himself. The forms of the *Code Duello* must be followed, however grievous the result. It was a civilized process.

Stefano had taken the fencing lessons required of his station in society, but he wasn't much of a fighter. He didn't want to hurt anyone. He preferred the smell of the flowers of field and forest to that of freshly spilled blood. The carnage he'd seen resulting from other people's duels appalled him. And of course there were the deaths. So many unnecessary deaths in tribute to the shallow fiction of honor, personal or familial.

"Tomorrow dawn at the traditional place, Castello di Arechi. It shall be swords." As the challenged party, choice of weapons was Stefano's prerogative. He chose what he knew, but with trepidation borne of true knowledge of the situation. The lieutenant was a soldier. Stefano was young and inexperienced.

"We shall bring our doctor, and you will provide your own," responded Bellitro. "Well, then… until tomorrow." He clicked his heels, made a slight bow, and went off to tell his principal, the bully Romano, about the next day's festivities.

The die was cast. Had Stefano not responded thus, he would have been besmirched as a coward, perhaps shamed into leaving Salerno or even Italy altogether. Reputations were destroyed so easily every day by gossip and mislabeling, but being branded as a coward was the worst of all. How could a man have respect for himself after denying the right to prove himself by trial in single combat? It didn't matter what the reason was. In Italian society of the nineteenth century, a challenge once made must be accepted.

The night was longer than any other in Stefano Davidi's life of 19 years. It had to be the anticipation, the self-examination, the doubt he felt in a successful outcome. He couldn't remember why they were going to fight. Some slight or other, real or imagined, a jocular comment passed in a tavern, something not worth fighting over, as usual. But that didn't matter now. Anxiety tossed Stefano about in bed. Sleep was impossible. The night dragged on.

By the light of an oil lamp, he checked his sword. It was a fashionable foil of the day, forged in Toledo, Spain, and the best that Stefano could find amongst his acquaintances and borrow for the unavoidable event. He could do nothing about his skills; he was either prepared or not. The day would tell, but dawn was slow in coming.

In this year, 1838, dueling was common in Italy. The nobility dueled, and as herd instinct will influence populations to levels of irrationality, the practice was emulated by other levels of society. True, there were incidents in which an insult demanded satisfaction, but the duel was also a way for bullies to make their reputations. This seemed to be one of those instances. It might be Stefano's first duel, but not the lieutenant's. He was a known brawler, a *bretteur* with several duels already on his scorecard and two deaths to his credit. Stefano was in grave danger, and even though the reason for the encounter was vague to nonexistent in his mind, he could not back down. It wasn't an option.

Through mist in the pre-dawn darkness, Stefano, his second Antionio Ravelli, and Doctor Nottino made their way to the dueling ground at Castello di Arechi. Many a duel had been fought there, many fighters wounded, and some killed. Perhaps there'd be other duelists waiting to fight this morning, a long line of willing killers and victims, the skilled and unskilled, the peaceful and hostile. But no, Stefano's group was the first to arrive and didn't have to wait for others to settle their differences.

The sun was slow in revealing itself that morning. Thick clouds were building to the east threatening torrents of Mediterranean rain, cold and pummeling. Would the fight be postponed, perhaps even cancelled because of the weather? Doubtful. For a pistol duel, perhaps, but only because open ignition systems didn't work in the rain. But swords? The fight would go on as scheduled.

Mario Bellitro and his principal, Lieutenant Agostino Romano, arrived and strode confidently across the dueling ground as the sky began to lighten behind the broken cloud cover. A doctor followed more slowly, reluctant to be involved, but money was money after all.

Stefano's second, Antonio Ravelli, greeted them. "We are ready, gentlemen. Prepare yourselves."

The Lieutenant and Stefano removed their heavy coats and stood ready, clothed only in shirts and trousers. Neither wore chain mail or any other contrivance that would deflect a thrust or bend a sword blade.

Equally exposed and vulnerable, they faced one another.

The Lieutenant stood erect, his military training evident. He was well-muscled, in excellent shape, and already bore several scars from duels he had fought and survived. He stretched his leg and arm muscles to loosen himself up as well as to ward off the morning chill.

Stefano the student seemed ill-at-ease. He shuffled his feet, looked around nervously, hoping the authorities would show up to stop the impending event. Technically, dueling was illegal, though very popular with the young and adventurous and among older folks who valued their dignity too highly and took themselves far too seriously. The society recognized that a duel was necessary when honor was threatened. Few duelists faced prosecution, even when there was a death, as long as the codified rules of *Code Duello* had been strictly adhered to.

The seconds met on neutral ground between the antagonists and examined the swords.

"These foils seem to be in order. The length is good and the same for both. Neither man has the advantage," said Ravelli.

"Agreed," Bellitro said. "Let's get to the business." Though a second, a mere factotum, he wanted the upper hand and tried to take control of the situation.

The seconds handed an inspected sword to each other, then each to his man. The principals felt the balance, the heft of their weapons, the flex of the blade.

A coin was flipped into the air. Bellitro won the toss and would give the go-ahead. He wasted no time. The combatants faced each other at the distance of two swords. Bellitro gave the order: "*In guardia... Avanti!*"

The duelists measured one another. They circled, they approached, they retreated, approached again. Their blades touched with sinister metallic clickings as they feinted and withdrew, feinted and withdrew.

The Lieutenant attacked, his form elegant and precise, his skills evident. Stefano beat the Lieutenant's blade aside and struck with his own. A clean miss. He retreated quickly... quickly enough to avoid another attack. Lunge, parry, again, and again. The sound of metal against metal rang in the cool morning air.

Attempting an upward thrust by coming in low, Stefano attacked again, but he missed his footing. The Lieutenant parried and returned the attack. His blade found an opening. The lunge was swift and successful. He gave the blade a little twist to widen the wound before pulling it back out of his victim.

"I am killed!" Stefano gasped as he fell to the ground with blood pulsing from his throat. His opponent's blade had pierced the carotid artery. His doctor rushed to the fallen boy, but could do nothing. With surprise rather than pain on his youthful face, the boy bled out and died quickly.

The Lieutenant stood back and coolly observed the boy lying on the ground in a spreading pool of bright red blood. He wiped the fresh blood off his blade with a handkerchief, sheathed the weapon, slipped into his coat, and left the dueling ground with his companions, off to a hearty celebratory breakfast.

It fell to Ravelli to bring the body home and inform Stefano's family: his father and older brother Alfonso.

Monday

My Freelance Life

My name is Benjamin S. Bones, and I'm a consulting genealogist. My business card says I'm an "Articulator of Family Skeletons." That'll give you an idea of my somewhat flippant attitude toward life in general. I like to laugh and, though I consider myself to be a curmudgeon, I tend to see my fellow humans' strivings to be pretty ridiculous much of the time. So I laugh. You might say that I'm laughing in self-defense simply to keep from going insane when I look around and see what my earthly companions have been up to. Sometimes I think I'm the only sane person on the planet; lots of other people probably have the same thought about themselves. Maybe we're all nuts.

But laugh as I might at human foibles, I take my genealogical work seriously, too seriously at times, but not as seriously as my clients seem to. I mean, I want to do a good job for them, a thorough and professional job, but it's difficult sometimes, and not because of the work itself. It's because of the people, the clients and the agendas they hide from me until it's too late to avoid the consequences. Weird happenings seem to coalesce around me, and I sometimes find myself in the center of someone else's vortex, someone else's tornado of deception, greed, or revenge. In the immortal words of that great Texas bluesman Lightnin' Hopkins, "You got to watch it… all the time."

I've always thought of myself as an honest, law-abiding citizen. I don't kill people, don't steal, don't flimflam people out of their stuff. When I work on someone's genealogical puzzle, I charge fairly and give my clients good value for the money I'm paid. In the business of genealogical research, reputation is most important. I want mine to be sterling.

I don't please everyone all the time, but they always get what they ask me to find, even though they may not want to hear the details and truth in the end. People show up with some strange requests, and the answers to their questions might not be what they're hoping for. I've had situations where they become absolutely homicidal about what I find for them in their family history, things that they don't want found… or bits that I don't find that they desperately want for one reason or another. There have been cases where I've discovered a jailed missing brother, a family history of serial killings, unexpected heirs… I'm sure you get the idea. It's a weird game that I find myself entangled in sometimes, and most of the time, not a game of my choosing.

But I can say that I'm a professional genealogist, and even if I don't have a regular job, I'm able to earn a living through freelance research work that comes to me via referrals from satisfied clients. This is no way to get rich, that's for sure, but at least I'm able to pay my monthly expenses and buy the fresh vegetables, turkey hot dogs and tofutti ice cream that I survive on in my bachelor life.

This particular case, which I call "The Twin Pistols," was full of surprises. The problems I encountered and the surprises that found me weren't clear at the beginning. They never are. It's only when the evidence begins to accumulate, and sometimes the bodies too, that the truth begins to show its teeth. That's when things get interesting.

"The Twin Pistols" sounded like a simple case at the beginning, but personal animosities made it a quagmire of jealousy, hatred and vituperation born of a father's decision over 200 years ago, a decision he thought would be the answer to the problem at hand: ownership of the set of dueling pistols that lay at the core of the family's history. Perhaps it was the answer; perhaps it was only one possible answer out of a myriad of choices. We can only operate on the facts we know at the moment. We make the best decisions we can. But somewhere down the road, more than 200 years later in this case, the decision had unforeseen consequences that maimed as if the well-meaning father's hand had struck a crippling blow through time.

And then there was the… but you'll find out about all that as the story unfolds. It all began with a letter…

The Arrington Letter

It was something of a shock when I received the letter on the fancy, heavy-duty stationery embossed with a seal and sporting raised printing from Arrington, Pettibone & Peak, LLC in Raleigh, North Carolina.

Much of the time, a letter from a law firm isn't going to bring good news. That might be a gross generalization, but think about it. When was the last time Uncle Bigbucks died and left you the keys to his bank safe deposit boxes full of cash in exotic locales around the world, the 22-bedroom mansion on his private island in the Bahamas, and the code word that opens the hidden vault in the bomb-proof basement bunker? Those are rare events indeed.

So when I retrieved the letter from my post office box, I was hesitant to tear into it. I took it home, tossed it atop the disorderly mess of papers on my desk, and decided to listen to some of Jimmy Yancey's mellow piano blues to calm my nerves. Maybe a Drambuie over ice would help. No, I'd better not. It was too early in the day.

A lawyer letter. I was nervous and sat down to think about opening it. It lay on the desk staring back at me. I knew it would have to be opened eventually, but I reacted just like any normal person would.

I'm like that sometimes. Let me explain.

To look at me, I'm an ordinary kind of guy: approaching 40, hair thinning a bit on top, too much booze, and I don't get the recommended amount of exercise or eat enough fresh fruit and vegetables. But I'm mostly functional and I'm not looking for any trouble. I keep a watchful eye on my finances, clean my own apartment and do my own laundry, floss daily, and I always wear a seatbelt.

But sometimes… sometimes the motivation to keep going drains out of me and I sink into an emotional morass. I suspect it's related to the drive-by shooting that killed my wife and unborn child years ago. Sure I grieved, but I'm probably not over it yet, nor will I ever be. That's the kind of life event that one never recovers from. An event like that sticks with you, haunts you day and night, receding when you're distracted by work or other business and roaring back when you have time to sit and contemplate the depths of the drink in your hand.

I wasn't down in my personal black hole at present, but with all those bills facing me and no active research project, things were looking bleak financially. I was balancing on the head of the proverbial pin, and there were no dancing angels in sight.

After looking at the envelope for a while, I finally worked up the courage to open it. Considering the state of the rest of my life, how bad could its contents be?

Guess what? It turned out to not be bad news after all. Instead, it was a job offer. It read as follows:

> Arrington, Pettibone & Peak, LLC
> The Arrington Building
> 85 Teasel Road SE, Raleigh, North Carolina
>
> Dear Mr. Bones,
> I got your name from a friend for whom you did a successful research job a while ago. She recommended you quite highly, not only for your technical competence and integrity, but for your absolute confidentiality as well.
> By way of introduction, I am an attorney in Raleigh. I'm also a gun collector, and it's in that area that I would like your help. There is a dueling pistol in my collection, a pistol that I did not collect. It's one of a pair, and it was passed down in my wife's family since the middle 1800s. I wish to reunite the set. Where is the other pistol? That is the question I would like you to answer for me.
> I hope this puzzle will be of interest to you. Whether it is or not, please contact me at your earliest convenience. If you will accept the challenge, we can set the parameters of the job at that time, though I'll tell you I'm willing to pay you a $10,000 research fee if you succeed, in addition to any expenses you might incur.
> I hope to hear from you in the affirmative.
> Sincerely,
>
> Wallace Davidi Arrington
> Attorney at Law

Wow! A job offer. And just in time, too. I wondered if I could get a cash advance from Himself.

A few words of explanation are needed. I'm not a hunter or a target shooter, not a firearms enthusiast at even the lowest level. Thus, I am fairly ignorant about guns. I know a gun can be a precision machine and sometimes even a jewel of metalwork artistry, but when you get down to fundamentals, the gun was invented to kill living things. The history of the gun is an ongoing tale of murder and mayhem. And the tale hasn't yet been fully told.

But I wasn't being asked to be a gun expert, was I? Not at all. For this job, I didn't need to know anything about guns, though I imagined I'd learn a great deal about guns and dueling in the course of my investigations, if I took the job. I'm a genealogist, and I was being asked to track down an object that was hidden somewhere in a family history. That was something I could do, knew how to do, and that I was skilled at doing. I was a veritable bloodhound of history and could follow a faint scent backwards through time until I found the… the "whatever" was being sought. I'd done it before and I would do it again. It was my bread and butter.

This request looked interesting for the challenge, the history, and the money. Did I mention the money?

I decided to do a bit of basic research on dueling pistols before calling Wallace Arrington, Esq. I wanted to mention the money to him, too. I did mention the money, didn't I?

Calling Wally

"So when can you start work on this?" Wallace Arrington, Attorney-at-Law, was a no-nonsense kind of guy.

Did I want to fake it or tell him the truth? Did I want to tell him I was frantically searching for work or make him think I was in more demand than I usually am? As a matter of fact, my date book was empty for the next several weeks except for tasks like paying off credit card debts, paying car insurance, paying the rent, paying, paying, paying. It got to me after a while, but that's the way my life is now and has always been. There's never quite enough in the coffers. His $10,000 would help greatly.

Arrington went on. "I've had another genealogist, a local woman, take a look at this problem, but she's much more a 'spiritual' airy-flairy type than a fact-based type of person, if you know what I mean. She didn't help me out on this."

"Really? What's her name? I probably know her. The professional genealogy community isn't all that big."

"Portella. Portella Elnora Bakkernon DeNight. What a name. She's got a listing in the Raleigh phone directory under 'Genealogists.' I never even knew they had that category."

"Yeah, I know her... know of her anyway. I hate to tell you this, but she's not highly regarded as a genealogist, though she's a skilled marketer and well known amongst the amateurs. She does quite well financially, as you probably found out."

"Yes, I learned that. She charged by the hour, not for the result. Good thing for her; not so good for me. I should've known better. She found a couple of people for me, but that was it." I could hear Arrington's mental gears through the phone connection as he remembered his Portella DeNight experience. "You were recommended by someone whose judgment I trust."

"Thanks for the ego builder," I told him. Since most of my work is done in isolation, any positive stroke feels great. "I took a quick look online at dueling before calling you... read a bit of history about duels. Those people were nuts!"

"I have to agree with that," Arrington said. "It was passed down from medieval knighthood and was the accepted way to right a wrong in those days. Nowadays we battle in the courtroom, but it can be just as destructive to a family's reputation and fortune."

He had reminded me. "Ahh, right... the money. By the way, you don't suppose I could get an advance on my fee, for expenses, that is..." Oops. I'd blown it. Too obvious. That's why I could never go into law or politics; I can't hide my true self under an emotionless mask. What I'm thinking has always been too easy for other people to read. And I tend to blurt out those thoughts.

"I don't see why not. But your expenses should be fairly low. I expect you to be our guest at my house. After all, you'll be working for me. And I'm sure you'll want to meet my family and familiarize yourself with my gun collection. I have a great cook, too. You should enjoy all that," he enthused.

"Oh, sure. Sounds like a great idea. All of it, I mean. But I have to admit at the beginning that I'm not a gun nut... er... enthusiast. My experience and knowledge in that area is seriously limited."

It amazes me how people with an enthusiasm for a topic expect other people to share their ardor. We may think we live in an ordered and civilized society, but the fact is that the human race lives a pure anarchy, with everyone rushing around in different directions vigorously pursuing their particular individual agendas. It's hard to get people to work together toward a common goal even if they all agree on the ultimate desired result.

Arrington tried again. "You haven't answered my question. When do you think you can start on this?"

I was hungry and approaching broke. My date book was clear. I could begin immediately, but I wanted to think about things and do a bit more backgrounding before I started on his family history.

"I could drive to Raleigh in a day or so if that would be convenient. Since I live in Asheville, it's only a 4-hour drive, even if I make a pit stop or buy gas."

"That'll be fine. How about tomorrow, Tuesday? I have several appointments in the morning, but we could have lunch at my favorite downtown place, *Caffé Luna*. We'll discuss our business arrangements and you could come back to the office with me to sign the contract."

"Contract? What contract?" I asked.

"I'll draw up a little agreement about the scope of the job. We can hammer out the finer points over lunch."

A contract, eh? Well, I was dealing with a lawyer here, wasn't I? Of course there'd be a contract. I wondered what it would say. "The party of the first part…" etc., etc. I saw that Marx Brothers movie, the one where Groucho and Chico are reviewing their contract, tearing off paragraphs until there's only the "sanity clause" left. I'd soon enough learn what my contract said, all "standard" boilerplate clauses, I'm sure.

There was no way to fight it. "Okay. Sounds good to me. Noon tomorrow at *Caffé Luna*. I can find it."

He ended the call and that was it. I had a job. Another search for a missing artifact. An antique gun this time. I hoped it wouldn't be like *The Search for Paneta's Crown* in which jealous siblings were killing one another to acquire the hidden spoils of a father's will. I had a few close calls in that adventure. But that's a story for another time.

Whistling a basic blues riff, I set about gathering the tools, reference materials and personal items I thought I'd need for the job.

1838 Paris, France

Tools of Death

Stefano's funeral was held after a short wake. It was expensive. This family, the Davidis, wasn't a religious family. Each family member had his own idea of what faith was, what it wasn't, and what it might or should be. They went to church only for the most important church events and attended funerals when necessary, but they were "free thinkers" for their time. They needed to be taught a lesson about their community responsibilities. The priest demanded more than the usual fee for his officiating.

The father, a shoemaker by trade, cried. His wife had died years before and now his youngest son was gone. Only his oldest son Alfonso and himself were left of his immediate family. At least Alfonso's wife was pregnant. The family would go on. They hoped, perhaps even prayed, for a boy child.

Alfonso was a studious one, the son studying chemistry at the university. Only in his early twenties, his future as a chemist compounding medicines would provide a good living for himself and his family. Alfonso Davidi could be quick-tempered when crossed, but he had never been involved in a duel. Clever and sometimes devious, he understood the value of patience and knew how to wait for opportunity to favor him.

And now his younger and inexperienced brother had been coldly killed, murdered by a practiced bully known in the region, a fire-eater, a *bretteur*. Alfonso wasn't much of a swordsman. Of a more intellectual turn of mind than many of his contemporaries, he'd neglected the art of fencing that so many younger men avidly pursued.

The grieving father and his lone remaining son sat over large cups of wine after brother Stefano's funeral. Neither brother had been a fighter. The father now feared for Alfonso. If something happened to him…

"I will redeem the honor of our family," Alfonso promised his father. "This murder cannot go unavenged. I will kill the *bretteur*."

"But how? You are no more a duelist than Stefano was. I don't want to lose you, too."

"I am going to Paris to buy the best guns I can find. I have a maker's name. By the time I return I will be an expert," he explained. He packed some clothes, some bread and cheese. And for good measure he tucked a stiletto down into his boot.

The distressed father couldn't stop his son. Determined to avenge the family's honor, Alfonso left their little house in Salerno. He was gone for two months.

Leaving his pregnant wife behind in his father's care, Alfonso left Salerno and headed north for France. Traveling by foot and sometimes riding in farmers' carts, he made his way north along the coast through the larger towns of Napoli, Roma, Livorno, Genoa and the many smaller towns between.

A month after starting out, tired and bedraggled, he crossed into France, made his way through the Alps to Grenoble, then across central France to his goal: Paris. He'd lost weight on the trip, this because he was hoarding the little money he had for the purchase of pistols. He could eat after his goals were accomplished.

Paris was even larger than Roma, and more cosmopolitan, but the people were generally friendly toward this Italian vagabond in their midst. The bread was good, the pastries delicious, the women beautiful and willing, but Alfonso was focused on his mission of revenge. He woke in the nights sweating and gasping, from cloying funereal dreams, his brother's dead face begging him to right the wrong that had been done to their family.

The furthest outskirts of Paris had a rural flavor. Slowly, the large estates and farms of the countryside gave way to smaller farms and occasional shops. There was a more international seasoning as well. Alfonso met people from other cultures: Arabs wrapped colorfully for the equatorial heat of their native lands, their shrouded women, Jews in their traditional black, loud bearded Germans speaking their guttural language and swigging flagons of beer, the occasional arrogant Englishman. And of course there were women. France was famous for its women even then. Some were selling fruits and vegetables, some sold baskets and other handmades, some were selling themselves. Human life was the same everywhere.

Alfonso asked around in his bastard French and was directed to 4, rue des Trois-Frères, the workshop of one François Prélat, a gunsmith of international renown. Alfonso had reached his destination. His goal was in sight.

The little shop was in a pleasant and unassuming building on a small street in Montmartre. It took him a while to find it, but eventually Alfonso sauntered past the shop, unsure of his next move. Determined on revenge, he had come a great distance to buy a weapon, but now that he was here… What to do?

He tried the door of the shop. It was unlocked. He entered and looked around as his eyes adjusted to the general gloom of the enclosed space.

The small front room of the shop was a showroom. There were guns hung on the walls: single pistols of various designs, a pair of facing duelers hung over there, several long guns on racks. On shelves to one side were some walnut gun boxes. One box was open to view and contained a beautifully-wrought pair of duelers inlaid in gold on their locks and barrels. Surely too expensive for this young man from Salerno.

A lean mustachioed man stepped from a curtained doorway and greeted him in French. Prélat himself? After only two weeks in the country, Alfonso's French was rudimentary. He was able to ask for bread, for wine, for a bed, to say "Thank you" and "Please," but he was not equipped for the detailed discussion he now had to have.

Without preliminaries, he said in a bastard French "I'm looking for a gun that will kill with one shot."

A naïve remark perhaps, whether understood or not. A shot's effect depended on where it entered one's adversary and the damage done by the projectile. Any gun will accomplish the task. The critical factor is where the gun is pointed; that depended on the skill of the practiced shooter with a true and well-crafted weapon in hand.

Their initial meeting was awkward because of the obvious language problems. But one doesn't go to a gunsmith for coffee and pastries. One goes to see a gunsmith about a gun. The purpose of Alfonso's visit was clear enough.

Prélat showed Alfonso a single pistol that he retrieved from a rack on the wall. He worked the lock, cocked the weapon and tripped the trigger, showed how the ramrod was stored conveniently in a slot below the barrel. The gun was plain but highly functional, expertly made and impressive, and would do a workman-like job all right. Alfonso was determined to kill his man, whether in a fair fight or not, and for this he needed a set, not a single. He held up one finger and shook it negatively in the air before the pistol maker. Alfonso then held up two fingers in an unmistakable and easily understood gesture. For emphasis, he pointed his index fingers at one another in front of him and worked his thumbs.

Prélat laughed, nodded, and smiling broadly, went to the shelf of gun cases. He had just completed work on a matched set of percussion dueling pistols for a client, but the gentleman had been killed in a street fight before he could pick up the commissioned work. Paris was a dangerous place, and not only because of the French penchant for the duel. The gentleman had been set upon in a dark street by thieves and stabbed to death for a handful of coins. The thieves, as usual, were never caught.

The gunsmith set a wooden box on a counter and opened it. Alfonso was dazzled. The pistols and all their accompanying accoutrements were ensconced in fitted compartments in the baize-lined box. The walnut box was exquisitely crafted, but it was nothing compared to the guns themselves.

The guns were made for a deadly purpose, but they were works of art, individually and collectively. The 10-inch octagonal barrels were decorated with gold foliate inlays at the muzzle, the tang, and where the stock wrapped around them. The lock plates and percussion hammers were similarly enhanced. The ebony grips swooped in smooth arcs downward from the barrels and lock mechanisms, and were intricately carved in a floral motif.

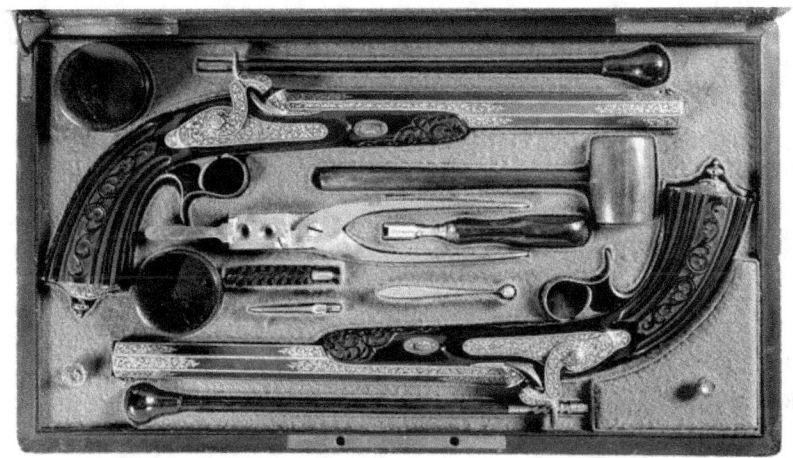

Alfonso reached out to lift one of the guns from the case, but hesitated and lifted his eyebrows at Prélat. The gunsmith edged the box closer to his potential customer and gave a nod.

With two hands, Alfonso picked one of the guns from its baize cavity, holding it as if it were a delicate bird egg. He hefted it gently in both hands, then took the pistol into his right hand and lifted it to eye level and sighted down the barrel, his arm straight out in front of him. The gun naturally came to a level shooting position. The weight was reassuring, the balance perfect. This was truly a masterpiece of murderous artistry.

Satisfied that he'd found what he was after, he set the gun back into its coffin and raised his hands in a "what now" gesture. He tapped the fingers of his right hand into the palm of his left in the universally understood sign for money.

To avoid confusion, Prélat grabbed a scrap of charcoal and a piece of wood and scratched out a number. It was a large number. Alfonso assumed that the Frenchman was writing in francs, and unsure of what his gold Italian coins were worth, decided to let the gunsmith see how much he'd brought.

Alfonso and his clothing may have looked worn from his month of travel, but he had brought his savings with him safely tucked away in his "casa forte," a small leather purse that he wore concealed next to his skin. He poured its contents out on the counter. Prélat picked up a coin and looked at it carefully. He thought a moment, then sorted the gold coins into two piles, one larger than the other. He pushed the smaller pile back toward

Alfonso, and pulled the other toward himself. The two men smiled. A deal had been struck. Alfonso had bought the dueling set.

Alfonso returned to Italy following the route he had come by, careful to protect the dueling set from jealous eyes and unscrupulous hands. These were to be the instruments of his revenge for his brother's unnecessary death. When he passed through wilder regions, he practiced loading and shooting his new guns. They were beautiful examples of the gunsmith's craft, but they were also easy to handle and frighteningly accurate. They provided him with many meals of campfire-roasted rabbit on the way home.

The year was 1838.

Tuesday

Caffé Luna

In North Carolina's capital city Raleigh, *Caffé Luna* is a fashionable Italian restaurant downtown. It's located around the corner from the law offices of Arrington, Pennington & Peak, LLC. As usual, I was early for my appointment, this time by half an hour. I'm always early. It comes from a fear of arriving late and missing the important stuff. Something must've happened to me along that line when I was a kid. I can't remember what it was.

Entering through a doorway catty-corner on the building, I found myself in a pleasantly airy and spacious peachy pastel eating space. Tables were arranged in orderly rows without any feeling of crowding. If the food was as nice as the feel of the place, I was in for a treat. But I had a nagging worry. I hoped Arrington would pick up the check. After all, it was his meeting. He'd called it.

A fit-looking mustachioed gentleman in a white dress shirt and tan slacks greeted me at the concierge desk. The major-domo, I guessed, but it turned out he was the owner. He picked up a menu from a stack on the cashier's counter and asked, "Hello. Is this your first time with us?"

"Uh… yes, it is. I'm supposed to meet someone here. A lawyer. Wallace Arrington. Is he here yet?"

"Wally? I haven't seen him. But I'll take you to his favorite meeting table."

I followed the gent through the restaurant to a small table. He pulled the chair out for me and asked, "Would you care for drink while you're waiting?"

I thought for a second, thought better of the suggestion, but not much more than fleetingly. "Drambuie, neat," I said, knowing it wasn't a good idea before a business meeting. But what the hell...

Drambuie was my nemesis, my favorite libation, my hobby, and probably my ultimate fate as well. One drink could easily lead to another, followed by another, then another, ending in regrets and a walloping headache the next day. The welcoming gent left for the bar to retrieve my drink while I sat there promising myself I'd only have one. By the time Wally arrived, I was on my second.

I rose to my feet and we shook hands. Wallace Arrington's grip was strong, but his hand was small, warm and soft, a lawyer's hand, a hand that could change lives with the stroke of a pen but wasn't too handy with a screwdriver. He stood about five feet tall, and his width was about two and a half feet, making him short and narrow front to back and wide when seen from the front, like a cardboard cutout of himself. He wore sharply-pressed gray slacks, a lavender dress shirt with a red and pink diagonally striped bowtie, a tan sport jacket, brown and white saddle shoes, and sported a wide smile of perfectly even white teeth. His eyes though, there was something... a shrewd look about them, like they were constantly analyzing everything that passed before the man. Lawyer's eyes.

Wally signaled Parker, *Caffè Luna*'s owner as it turned out, for another round for me and something for himself. I was in trouble.

"Glad you could make it," Wally Arrington, Esq. said, his voice a deep basso with rumblings of important lurking issues that he was aware of but you had no clue about. "You'll like this place. Very comfortable. Quite friendly. Excellent cuisine. I come here often."

I wondered who was paying for my drinks. Whoever it was had better cut me off. One was enough, two was sufficient, three was more than plenty. It's not will power that counts in these situations; it's won't power. I took a sip. What the hell...

Wally reached into the inside pocket of his sport jacket. "Here's a picture of the gun in my possession." Wally laid a professional quality photograph on the table in front of me. "Alfonso Davidi acquired a set of dueling pistols from the maker, one François Prélat, a Parisian gunsmith. Alfonso killed two men with the guns to avenge his brother's death, in legitimate if illegal duels of course, after which he fled to England. When he died, he split the set between his twin boys. That was in the late 1800s. The gun was passed down from descendant to descendant through the years, and I ended up with this one via my marriage to Celine, his great-great-granddaughter by blood. Wait 'til you see it in person. It's a pip!"

The photo was good, the lighting superb, but the gun itself was exquisite. It was made of a dark metal and was copiously decorated with gold inlays over all the metal parts. The quality of workmanship was obvious even to me in my gun-ignorant and slightly inebriated state.

"It might have been my having this one," he continued, "but I've become something of a firearms collector over time. Not an expert, you understand, nor a sharpshooter. I don't shoot the damn things. They're dangerous. I'm merely a collector, mostly of flintlocks and older percussion arms. But having only the one gun of this dueling set and none of the accompanying gewgaws that go with the set has always bothered me. Besides, we're talking family history here." He sipped his drink and waved the restaurateur back to our table. I hoped he wouldn't call for another round. He did.

We ordered our lunches. I ordered the *Penne Cappesante*, a remarkable dish of penne pasta, scallops, and spinach sautéed with garlic and olive oil. There was no question about it; this was a great restaurant. The chef was a master.

Wally ordered the grilled salmon with vegetables, saying that it was his favorite and regular lunch in that it provided a healthy diet for a man of his girth. Laughing, he slapped his side with an open hand for emphasis, producing a sound like whacking an empty barrel.

After we'd ordered, several suited downtown fellows stopped at our table to greet Wally. They looked like businessmen, but they could've been politicians as well. We were in the state capital, after all. Those guys all tend to look similar what with their nondescript suits and trendy but similar silk ties. There was a round of hand-shaking. One of the men leaned down and whispered something in Wally's ear. Wally's forehead creased as he listened.

"Don't worry about it, Garnet. I told you I'd handle it. Just be patient and don't get your drawers in a knot. These things have to be handled delicately. They take time to work out so everyone is satisfied. You have the money handy, right?"

The man addressed as Garnet flashed a suspicious glance at me. He looked familiar. Wait a second. I was in Raleigh, the state capital. This guy was a member of the state senate or something. I'd seen him on TV making promises to save us all from the threats of international terrorism, sinners and atheists, abortion rights and the confiscation of our holy guns. Not a guy I'd vote for.

The man addressed as Garnet leaned over and tried to whisper in Wally's ear again. Unfortunately, he had one of those professional announcer voices that cut through the din and confusion of ambient sounds. I heard every word clearly. "Any time you need it... but the judge..."

Arrington cut him off with a raised hand. "Don't worry. I've got it."

Seeming only marginally reassured, Garnet and his look-alike companion, whether his factotum or his equal, left us to our meal. The companion had said nothing through the entire exchange. He had stood and continuously scanned the restaurant and the street outside the large windows. I decided he was security.

"Politicos. They're always worried about... well, I'd best not say." And with that, Wally turned his attention back to our business. "How long do you think it will take for you to find the gun?"

"It all depends..." I started.

He interrupted. "Wait a minute. You stole my line. That's a lawyer's answer." He roared at that, impressed with his own witticism.

I smiled politely, unimpressed. He'd asked me a question and I'd given him the most direct answer I could. I wasn't sure I liked the guy. And a lawyer, too. Past experience ruled; I probably shouldn't trust him too far either.

"Sorry, but that's the correct answer, Mr. Arrington."

"Call me Wally, please. Everyone does. I may be an attorney, but deep down under the leathery exterior I'm a pretty flexible guy, just like an ordinary person." He took a sip of his drink and gave me a rather focused and lawyerly look. "I'll accept that as a legitimate answer. What's involved in your process? How's it going to go?"

"You haven't given me enough info on what we're looking for yet. I need more details. I mean, I have a basic plan, but that's all."

I'd given some thought to how to proceed before coming to Raleigh and I had a rough plan of attack. The track I'd have to follow traced his wife's branch of the family back in time to when the matched pistols were divided between Alfonso's twins, then following the other branch forward in time until I either discovered whether they still had the gun or had sold it off. If it had been sold, I would have to track the sale and any subsequent sales until I found the current owner.

The search was pretty straight-forward, at least in theory. Of course, there would be obstacles to encounter along the way. There were technical obstacles like breaks in the line of traceable document evidence, marriages of family women with accompanying vexing name changes, and there were always people who didn't want you to find what you're after, though in this case I couldn't see a reason why anyone would object. There are sometimes secret agendas, some of which might be revealed after a while, and some that would always remain hidden but would effect the search. You never knew what you'd find when starting out.

And with all of that, half of my search would be in Great Britain, where I knew little about available genealogical resources. My work was a varied and challenging detective game.

Arrington leaned his bulk forward eagerly. His move shoved the table foward several inches. He made a gimme gesture with his half-folded hand. "So…"

"I know I have to trace your family, er… your wife's family, that is, back to where the guns were divided up. I suspect that will be in Merry Olde England, but I'll know for sure when I find the bifurcation. Then I have to come forward in time again tracking the provenance of the weapon. Sounds simple, doesn't it? Well, it's not. It takes lots of digging and it takes as much time as it takes."

Arrington didn't answer, not in words anyway. He just sat, drink in hand, giving me that basilisk stare of his.

"Now, what can you tell me that will help focus the search? Tell me about the family, the family legends, anything you happen to know."

Arrington took a gulp of his drink, rubbed his hands together, and dug into the story. "The family story is that her distant forebear, Alfonso Davidi, acquired a matched set of dueling pistols before he migrated from Italy to England. This was back in 1838 or so. His younger brother had been killed in a sword duel and Alfonso bought the pistols to revenge his brother in the most modern manner available to him at the time. He fought two duels with the guns, duels in which he killed his brother's killer and another man. He fled Italy soon after and settled near London. When Alfonso died, his will split the matched pistol set between his twin boys Carlo and Armond. Primogeniture was strong in those days, but Alfonso probably wanted each son to have a piece of the family history that had brought them out of Italy."

"Interesting," I said. "I've run into primogeniture problems in my work before. Those folks back then did what they did with no thought about the future effects of their decisions. It was a simpler time."

Wally went on. "The pistols were made in Paris by François Prélat. Nowadays, a matched set of Prélat percussion dueling pistols might bring between $20,000 and $45,000 at open auction. But I'm not interested in the money. As Armond's lineal descendant, by marriage if not by blood, I ended up with one pistol of the set, but the other pistol, along with the original gun case and the various accoutrements, is out in the world somewhere. I don't know what happened to the family branch that descended from brother Carlo. The pistol might still be held by someone in that genealogical line or it might have been sold off. I don't have a clue as to its whereabouts."

Wally studied me with that canny legal eye again. "So you won't give me a time estimate?"

"I can't. It'll take as long as it takes."

He leaned back in his chair until it creaked. "What about *Ancestry.com*? Wouldn't that be an easier way to gather your information? It'd be faster, too, wouldn't it?"

I gave him my stock analysis of the online amateur genealogy situation. "It would be if the information there was reliable. Unfortunately, there are too many amateurs out there. Much of their info was gathered by casual family genealogists with no idea about provenance or original sources. The info is sometimes disorganized, redundant or incomplete, with sources largely not cited. I'm better off following trails of my own devising. I like to go to the original sources to find my documents. Believe me; I know what I'm talking about."

He chewed on that for a minute. I could hear the gears in his lawyer mind churning, trying to grind my explanation up into easily dissected unconnected pieces for analysis. But he was a man who also had to follow trails of evidence in his own profession, and he accepted my explanation as valid.

We finished our meal, knocking off a $45 bottle of wine on top of the preliminary drinks. When we were done and the table had been cleared, Arrington rose. "Let's go up to my office. I've got a contract for you to sign."

"Don't we have to pay for lunch?" I asked naively.

"Don't worry about it," he said. "I have a running tab here. I pay once a month."

And off we went… to lawyer-land.

Wally Arrington's offices were tangible proof of his legal success. There was dark wood paneling everywhere, tasteful original artworks on the walls even in the reception area, and people incessantly going back and forth on what looked like vitally important business missions. Everyone was dressed to the nines, as they say, as if the prom would officially begin as soon as the band arrived.

In the Big Man's office, he went behind his glass-topped wooden desk and I sank into a comfy leather chair facing him. He opened a folder and slid it across the desk for me to sign.

"Can I read this first?" I asked, being the paranoid wise-acre I am.

"If you want a lawyer to interpret it for you, I'll have one of my interns come in to help," he joked. "It's not too complex. If you can't understand it, you're not my man for this job."

I looked at the document. It was only a single sheet, and only two thirds of that. In the simplest legalese it read:

Research Agreement Between
Wallace Arrington and Benjamin S. Bones

It is agreed that:

1. The goal of this agreement is to determine the location of the second gun of an 1838 set of matched Prélat dueling pistols. One pistol of this set is now in Wallace Arrington's possession.

2. Benjamin S. Bones, Genealogist, will undertake this research task.

3. Wallace Arrington agrees to pay all expenses incurred in this research up to a limit of $5,000. Additional expenses must be approved by Wallace Arrington before being incurred.

4. Upon successful completion of the research task (finding the second gun of the Prélat set), Wallace Arrington will remit a $10,000 research fee to Benjamin Bones, as well as reimbursement for any outstanding expenses.

5. Wallace Arrington will handle all negotiations for acquisition of the gun, and he will be responsible for the final purchase.

6. All research materials and notes, and the results discovered will become the sole property of Wallace Arrington.

Wallace Davidi Arrington	Benjamin S. Bones
Attorney at Law	Genealogist & Researcher

Have I mentioned the money? Times were hard and this research fee would make a big dent in my current financial difficulties. I grabbed the pen he held out to me and almost signed the paper.

But I had several thoughts.

"Look, Wally, if I find the gun, why don't I talk to the owner about buying it? I can handle it. I'll probably be right there face-to-face with him… or her."

Arrington puffed up a bit. Some color rushed to his pallid face. "No way. I'll do all the negotiating. I don't want you screwing things up."

"But I…"

Arrington cut me off. "That's my final word on it. I've had too many things go wrong at the last minute because of a lousy word choice or an added demand by one side or the other. I won't take the chance."

What could I do? It was his job and his money. He was the boss and could call the shots as he saw fit. Besides, that was one less wrinkle for me to worry about. But there was one more item I wanted to add.

"Look, I'm a bit short. Can I get an advance?" I asked.

"You haven't done anything yet," my employer responded.

"I know, but… call it an advance against expenses. I can't be here in Raleigh with empty pockets."

He laughed. "Things aren't that bad, are they?" He laughed again, sort of a chortle, but reached into the inside pocket of his sport jacket and pulled out a checkbook. He placed it on the desk in front of him and began to write. "Will $1,000 be enough?

"Yes, that'll be great."

He finished writing, tore the check out, and handed it to me. "I wouldn't normally do this, but you seem like a legit sort."

"Thanks." I took the check, folded it, and stuffed it down into my jeans pocket. "There's something else. I sometimes like to write up my genealogical adventures for publication. I'd like to have the right to do that."

Wally agreed immediately. "I have no problem with your future publication. I'll get one of my people to add that." He picked up a Mirado Black Warrior #2 pencil, thought for a second as he tapped it against the edge of his desk, then wrote.

"How's this sound: 'Number 7 – Benjamin Bones shall have the right to prepare his researches and the results in this matter for publication.'" Having scribbled the note, he handed it and the agreement to a minion who had appeared silently by his side at some secret signal. Had the minion been listening to our entire conversation? Was his private office wired *a la Nixon*?

He gave his instructions: "Add this line to this agreement and get two copies back to me right away."

The worker went off in a rush, returning in a few minutes with the copies of the revised document.

Arrington signed. I signed. I had a $10,000 job, and $1,000 in expense money in my pocket. There would be hurdles ahead to leap, but I was a practiced genealogical athlete. I was sure I could accomplish the task.

After insisting that I be his house guest while in Raleigh, Arrington gave me directions to his home. Did I detect a meta-agenda? Having now met the man and having a taste of his personality, I thought he probably wanted to keep tabs on his investment and the progress I would be making. He was a lawyer after all, and a bit paranoid for that. It was professional training and cynicizing experience that informed his view of the world, the people in it, and how it all worked. Let him think what he would. I would be happy to save the hotel money, even if he would have picked up the tab. Over the years, I'd discovered that concern for a client's assets was always appreciated by them, no matter how well-heeled they might be. In fact, the more money they had, the less they wanted to spend a penny that wasn't necessary.

Setting the Stage

With the contract finalized and signed by the parties, that would be by Wallace Arrington, Esq. and ye olde Benjamin S. Bones, I thought about heading back to *Caffé Luna* for a celebratory Drambuie. I could sit and think of how to proceed, maybe have another drink or two, then head over to Arrington's place for the night. By then I'd have an idea or several, a clear research plan, or at least the skeleton of a plan. After all, I was the "Articulator of Family Skeletons," wasn't I? *Live up to it, Bones.*

Looking at the problem with my experienced professional eye, I saw that this job promised to run in a straight line through history, first backwards to when the family split way back in England, and then forwards down the British branch to my goal... if, that is, if the gun we sought was still in the family. If the gun had been sold out of the family, it should be simple enough to track it from owner to owner. Antiques tended to carry their provenance with them as they traveled from hand to hand. There might be branches this way and that, but I expected this to be one of those linear jobs without any danger to myself or anyone else. Some jobs I'd had in the past included ambulance rides, hospital expenses, and on one job, a new car to replace the one that was run off the road. This job didn't have that sort of feel about it.

Arrington scribbled his home address on a sheet of monogrammed note paper. Handing me the paper, he said, "I've told my house staff you'll be staying with us for a few days, so they'll be expecting you. Just knock on the door."

"I need to ask... Can I get online at the house? I do a lot of digging on the Internet."

"Oh, certainly. There's wi-fi there and Simmy will give you the access code." He chuckled. "How did we ever get along without the Internet? Even a geezer like me."

"Simmy? Who's that?"

"That's our housekeeper, Simmy Whittington. She'll help you out with anything you need. Just ask." Arrington paused, then added, "Celine, that's my wife... she might be there too, though she comes and goes as she pleases. I doubt she'll be much help with any of this. She runs her life on her own agenda. It rarely includes me."

"Thanks for the info, for the work… and the accommodations."

"It's not all altruism. With you staying at the house I'll be able to keep a weather eye on what you're up to. I'd like daily reports on your progress."

It felt a bit like third grade in elementary school. I don't care for clients leaning over my shoulder watching my every move. Too much like a regular Dilbert cubicle job in the corporate world with a pushy overseer cracking the proverbial whip. But he was the boss.

"We'll need to do a basic interview on your family history," I told him. "That'll give me a baseline starting point. I can take it backwards from there. Can we do that this evening?"

We were interrupted at that point by another of Arrington's minions sticking her head in the office door. "Your 2 o'clock appointment is here, Mr. Arrington. And she's hot about something."

Arrington blinked himself out of his gun reverie and back into his day-to-day reality.

"Oh, all right. Look, Bones, I'll talk to you this evening. I should be home by 7 or 8. Will that do? Right now I've got to get back to earning a living. This bitch always has some problem or other, usually small stuff, but it keeps the cash flowing."

A living? It looked like this guy was already a king. A king. How much money does a king need? How many houses can a king live in; how many cars can a king drive at once; how many boats can a king race simultaneously? But that was his way down a gilded road of life that I've never understood, never experienced, and probably never will. My way was shuffling along a dirt track clinging to the side of a mountain and vying with carnivorous goats for the right-of-way. Different strokes, eh?

I got up to leave but Arrington had another thought. "By the way, there's an antique auction tomorrow afternoon and there are several guns on offer. I'm planning to go and you'll of course go with me."

"Yeah, sure. That'll be interesting, if not informative. You never know what you'll find. I always stop at garage sales, too."

He laughed as I left the palatial paneled office and headed back to *Caffé Luna* to celebrate my revised, if only temporarily, way of life. I reminded myself not to get used to it.

Home, Sweet Home, But Not Mine

The rest of that afternoon is a bit vague, as far as my memory. I remember that I wandered around Raleigh for a while and had a Drambuie at *Caffé Luna*, but I don't know how many more I had or where I might have had them. I'm sure it was more than the one I remember and probably less than six. I usually run out of cash before I run out of capacity.

I remember seeing a bit of downtown Raleigh, and thinking that the town thought a lot of itself. There were sidewalks on both sides of all the streets, and traffic lights at every intersection. It was the state capital, after all. Why shouldn't it be proud, perhaps a bit arrogant? Just look at all the remarkable decisions the state legislature made over the years. North Carolina has made history on numerous occasions and is known around the world for some of them. Nonetheless, every once in a while I'd see a guy pushing a shopping cart containing all his worldly chattels, or see a grizzled guy with a hand-lettered cardboard sign that read something like: "Down on my luck. God bless."

Anyway, I may have stopped because I was running out of cash. Maybe I was hungry. Maybe I found a library and went inside to look around. Like I said: "…that afternoon was a bit vague."

I found my way back to Parker's restaurant where I'd left my car before lunch. I make it a rule to never drive after I'd had a drink or two, but I wanted to keep my computer and notes close, so I decided that I'd risk the few blocks to Arrington's.

Guided by my GPS unit, I somehow ended up at the address Wally had given me on that sheet of fancy monogrammed paper. There was no cash left in my pocket, only a few coins, but I still had his check intact. I parked on the street out front. It wasn't my most skillful parking job.

My knock on Arrington's front door was answered by a stooped, 5-foot tall, grey-haired woman with ancient wrinkled skin the color of caramel. An aromatic cloud of laundry detergent surrounded her. Two Dobermans sat attentively on their haunches behind her in the hallway.

"Yeah? You Mr. Bone'?"

I nodded. "The name's Ben Bones. How do you do?"

"All right. Mr. Bones then." Her voice was strong, not that of a withered old woman. I heard a hint of the islands mixed in with a North Carolina drawl. "I'm Simmy." She turned back into the house. "Follow me."

No welcome, no small talk, no move to pick up my computer case or my little travel bag as house staff might be expected to do. I hefted my gear and followed the bent little woman. The bookend pair of sentinel Dobermans followed us. They cocked their heads at me, as if trying to work out who I was and what my role in their lives would be. Would I be a benefactor with bacon biscuits, or simply fresh prey? It seemed an open question.

The foyer expanded into a hallway facing a staircase that swept away in two arcs up to a mezzanine. A massive chandelier hung above the entry hall, but the place was bright with end-of-day sunlight streaming down through a skylight roof. No need for electric light just yet.

She showed me around cursorily: the library just off the hallway where she said I could plug in my computer and get on line, several bathrooms, a dining room with a table that could accommodate perhaps a dozen people, my bedroom upstairs. Nice place. Very comfortable, even if a bit crowded with statuary on pedestals everywhere you looked, several suits of armor, weapons tastefully hung on the walls, crossed halberds and such. It was a man's castle; I didn't see much I'd characterize as the result of a woman's touch. Didn't Celine The Wife live here, too?

Simmy silently abandoned me on my own in an upstairs bedroom and left with the dogs. I threw my suitcase onto the huge canopied bed and started to unpack. How long would I be staying? Undetermined. I didn't know the scope of the problem yet, did I? It's kinda hard to estimate without any facts. I tested the bed. Hard yet giving at the same time. That's all I remember.

Wally Arrington arrived home that evening at 7:30. He stormed into the house yelling for a sandwich and a drink. I was awakened and stuck my head out of my bedroom to watch the tableau in the hall below me. Simmy stepped out into the hall from her kitchen domain.

"Quit your hollerin' and come on in my kitchen, you ol' boar you." I learned later that that was a standard sort of greeting between them. They'd been together a long time. Master and servant, they had become friends over the years.

Thoroughly awakened by the noise, I came out of my room, trooped down the spiraling stair, and joined them in the kitchen. I had a bit of a headache.

"How about a beer, Ben?"

Ah, the cure for any headache: anesthesia. "Sure. Any time. What have you got?"

Wally took a bite of the meaty-looking sandwich Simmy had plunked down in front of him on the kitchen's central island and waved his hand to show I should open the refrigerator and look for myself. I did and selected a European import I hadn't heard of before, something from Croatia in an oversized bottle. Simmy appeared silently at my side with a similar sandwich for me, a bottle opener that she applied dexterously, and a glass into which she poured the beer without raising a foamy head. I could tell she'd done this before. Finished with me, she set a whiskey down next to Wally's sandwich platter.

"So what did you find out today? Anything exciting that I need to know?" He took a slug of his drink and gave me a piercing look.

"To tell the truth, I've been taking a nap since Simmy showed me to my bedroom."

"I expected more from you" he blustered. "What am I paying you for?"

"The fact is that you're not paying me anything actually. Besides that bit of expense money, I only get paid if I find something, remember? That's the essence of the deal that you set up. How and when I accomplish the task is my own affair. You're a lawyer, right? Then you should know that I'm an independent contractor, not an employee. How I accomplish the task is my own affair."

Realizing he'd caught himself in his own little trap, he backed off a hair. "All right. You've got me there. Look, I'm out of here early tomorrow morning for court and we'll do the auction in the afternoon, but I want to introduce you to the Prélat this evening. Are you up for that?"

"Sure. That's why I'm here, right?" I winked at Simmy just then, hoping to establish a touch of the rapport that I'm famous for. No response. Wally noticed, but I guess he didn't see the humanity of my attempt. At least he didn't acknowledge it.

Half an hour later, after my second beer and his third glass of brown liquor and with refreshed drinks in hand, Wally led me into the main hall and toward the back of the house.

It was an older brick house, not old enough to be a national historic monument, but old enough to have been built well by people who knew their business. They were craftsmen back then, and not just labeled as carpenters and brick-layers. It had probably been built between the wars. You know, between The War to End All Wars and World War II. And it was safe to assume that many of the artisans involved were killed fighting Hitler and his thugs.

There was a heavy oak door toward the end of the hall which Wally opened with a key he pulled from his pocket. "Simmy has an extra key," he told me. "You can use it any time you need to during your stay if you think it will help, but you can't take it out of the house, share it with anyone, or copy it. Just give it back to Simmy when you're done."

"No problem there," I answered, "but tell me more about the gun. What exactly am I looking for?"

"I'm going to do better than that. I'll show you the one I have. It'll be easy enough for you to recognize its mate when you encounter it."

"When," he'd said, not if, I thought. He had faith in my investigative prowess, but I was never completely certain I would succeed when beginning an assignment. This one seemed straight-forward, but it would be tricky. I'd been lucky in my career so far, but it didn't serve to be smug. I would certainly be able to track the

family members involved, but the gun itself was another matter. I could probably track it to its final owner, but beyond that anything was possible. It might have been sold at private auction to a secretive Japanese collector, been destroyed in one of the European wars between the 1800s and now, or been thrown into a garbage can as a nuisance family artifact. That would put a final dead end to the search. We'd see.

The door swung open and a light came on automatically illuminating a staircase that led downward in an industrial concrete shell. He descended and I followed. I had a flash thought of Poe's *The Cask of Amontillado.* It turned out that I wasn't too far off.

"This was a wine cellar when I bought the house," Wally explained like a tour guide. "The guy I bought it from was a connoisseur. Had thousands of dollars in rare wines down here, but you weren't allowed to drink any of 'em. I had air conditioning installed and set the place up for my gun collection. The place is pretty well bomb-proof. I think you'll be impressed."

I was impressed. The gun room lay behind a second oaken door which swung open to reveal a room with a footprint that was easily half the floor space of the house above. The walls were hung with all sorts of guns: pistols, rifles, a few extremely old looking pieces such as flintlocks and Arabesque matchlocks. Informative plaques accompanied each weapon. The central open floor space was set up with display cases vertical and horizontal, each with unique guns of various designs, guns that had been made with special purposes in mind, assassinations and the like. We humans are quite creative when it comes to inventing better ways to kill our fellows. For an historian, this room was a proper place to linger for hours.

Wally Arrington seemed to have become bigger, but it was only his pride that had puffed up. This collection represented years of searching and untold thousands of dollars spent on acquisition, not to mention the cost involved in setting the room up to museum standards.

"Wow!" I muttered.

"Yes, indeedy. I'm quite proud of all this. But I'd give it all up for the brother pistol to my Prélat. There's something about having a personal interest in it that won't let me rest."

"But you're not even related to family by blood, only by marriage."

He ignored my observation and walked to a glass-topped horizontal display case. "Here it is. What do you think?"

I looked. My mouth dropped open. I was astonished.

Resting centrally on the plain dark green velvet that lined the locked case was a work of exquisite metal craftsmanship. The dark iron of the 10-inch octagonal barrel was inlaid along most of its length in gold vegetative design that looked somewhat Arabic. The lock mechanism was similarly inlaid, the workmanship throughout precise, beautiful, and of the highest quality. The pistol's "furniture," its wooden parts, the stock and grip, were cleverly carved ebony, carved in a manner that would provide positive grip in a sweaty and nervous duelist's hand.

Prélat had obviously been a metalworking genius, a craftsman of the highest skills. I could understand why Arrington, beyond his assumed familial attachment, would have been in love with the piece strictly as a work of art and craft.

"Wow," I said again.

"That's what I say to myself every time I look at the damn thing. It's become an obsession for me. You can see why. It's not just my family's history. This thing is a jewel, don't you think?"

I did and told him so. "Yes, an amazing craftsman's distillation of humanity's propensity to murder."

Wally looked at me disapprovingly.

"Well, isn't it?" I challenged. "Sure it's beautiful, but its ultimate purpose is sinister. It's made to kill someone… to kill someone up close and personally."

"In the abstract, you're right, of course." He had to agree. "But…"

"Abstract, hell. That's why it was made. The fashion in those days was to call someone out, go to a quiet spot, and blaze away at one another until one of the combatants lay on the ground in a fatal condition. I've done my research. I know what this is all about." He couldn't fool me with his obfuscating lawyer's hyperbole. Not about this.

Wally put his hands up with palms facing me. "All right, you win. It's a killing machine. I admit it." He turned back to the display case. "But look at the workmanship, the delicacy of the inlay, the…"

"Okay, I get it. We're both right."

And with that both of us turned off the heat, at least for the moment.

I thought for a second, then asked a dumb question. "Has this thing ever been fired at anyone?"

"Absolutely. According to the family legend, the gun killed at least two men back in the 1800s… this gun or its missing companion. Does that bother you?" he asked with a wry smile.

"A bit. But regardless of what I might think on the editorial side, I'll do my best to find the other one. You can bet on that. That's what I do. I'm a professional."

He nodded approvingly, then turned to a tall bookshelf against one wall and pulled out a black, 3-inch thick loose-leaf notebook. Setting it gently onto the glass-topped display case, he opened it reverently, like it had a religious significance for him. He leaned toward me over the book as if to share a private communication.

"I've done considerable research on the guns and their maker, François Prélat. He was one of many gun makers of his time, the middle 1800s, and highly respected. Dueling was quite the fashion in Europe back then and there was a demand for high class instruments. Now that you've seen the gun, you know something of the quality of his work. It's a work of art as well as a tool for killing a man, as you so delicately pointed out." He laid his pudgy hand gently atop the fat binder on the table. "This notebook has everything I've found on the man and his work. You'll want to spend some time reading it."

"Definitely. That'll be very helpful."

And then he told me something about his family history.

"My name, Arrington that is, is not the family name you'll be looking for. I'm not descended by blood from the original owner of the guns, a character named Alfonso Davidi. Alfonso left

Salerno, Italy in the mid-1800s after killing two men in pistol duels with the Prélats. He was avenging his younger brother's death. That much I already know, though not much else. Davidi is my middle name now, but I had to shoehorn it in there myself after I married into the family. My wife resents the facts that I adopted the name and that I'm after the gun that I feel so possessive about. I don't know what's with her. She didn't give a hoot about it all her life. Then suddenly, when I became interested, she gets all worked up about it." He shook his head in exasperation.

"So who were your parents... and your wife's? She's the true Davidi by blood, right?"

"Right. My parents don't matter at all in this. Celine was born Arley, and her mother was a true Davidi descendant. That much I know, and her momma had the gun that I've got now. It was her dad, Adam Arley, who got me into the gun collecting thing in the first place. That was quite a few years ago. Celine never cared about the Prélat gun or any other weapons. Maybe it's a 'guy' thing," he said with a shrug. "Anyway, since he got me started, she's had an attitude about me and the guns. But hell, it was her choice in the first place. It was just another piece of old family junk to her, an inconvenience because of its weight every time she found a new place to live and had to move it. Now she's all bent out of shape about it. Been that way for years."

He took a swig of his whiskey.

I took a sip of my beer and thought abut the oddnesses that life throws at people. I wondered how Celine and Wally had gotten together in the first place. It was none of my business... but on the other hand, I'm a genealogist and it's definitely my business. So I asked.

"How did you and Celine hook up?"

"It was all her dad's fault. He was a lawyer, y'know, with a successful practice here in Raleigh. I was a young lawyer on the make, fresh out of law school. Adam and I met in court and immediately became friends. You know how that goes sometimes; you meet a guy and have some kinda instant connection. So he says, 'Come on over to my place tonight. I'm throwing a little soiree for some of the boys in the back room. You should meet them. It'll be good for your career.' Well, I went and met some of the local players, but I also met his daughter Celine. She was a real beauty back then, not the low-hanging rotten fruit on the tree she is today. That was the fateful evening. Her dad wanted a son-in-law with prospects. With his help and some borderline deals, I got plugged into the local scene. It's been downhill for almost 30 years since."

"You have an interesting way of putting it. Don't you like the law? Don't you like practicing law? The crucible of the courtroom? The prestige? The money?"

A disgusted look crossed his face. His brow furrowed.

"You have no idea what it's like in the trenches. There's lots of 'good old boy' deals going on all the time, and I found myself right in the middle of some pretty shady stuff right away. I stayed as honest as I could, but there's a taint to some of the work that you wouldn't believe. Everything's legal, mind you, but so close to the edge that you can feel the breeze as old Damocles' sword swings by just beyond your neck. You play along, make lots of money, lose little pieces of yourself along the way. The sharply defined principles of your youth get dulled bit by bit. After a while, you don't even notice." He pulled back and polished off his drink.

"You want something a little stronger?" he asked. "Every time I reminisce I feel I want a stronger moral anesthetic," he said honestly.

He returned to the bookcase, opened a concealed compartment that I hadn't noticed, retrieved a bottle and poured himself four fingers of a bourbon I didn't recognize the name of, slugged down half of it, then refilled his glass. He held the bottle and a glass out to me with raised eyebrows. I could see it was going to be a long, tough evening.

Strategizing

Back upstairs and comfortably ensconced in his library with refreshed drinks in hand, we continued our discussion.

"I guess you've already looked around in the gun collector's world, antique weapon auctions and such, but I'd like to take another look, maybe even take an advertisement or two in the various gun publications. You all right with that?"

"That's been done," Arrington said, "but it won't hurt to try again. Someone who didn't see the earlier ads may spot it this time around. I'll get one of my office staff to take care of it. They did it last time and still have the list of places to post in magazines and online."

"What about museum collections? Antique dealers? Have you looked there?"

Arrington shook his head negatively. "Never thought about museums. I've always assumed the gun would still be in the family. I thought that whoever owned it now would have the same fascination with it as I do. Dumb assumption for a lawyer to make. I'm not supposed to assume things without investigating the facts behind them, and then to consider situations from all angles. That's your basic due diligence. I'll put my people on that, too. It's great being able to send people off on various missions. Covers lots of ground in less time."

He was quiet for a minute, considering his options, I supposed. And then he changed course.

"I've got court tomorrow morning, but I'm planning to take us both to that auction tomorrow afternoon. I keep track of auctions around Raleigh, but I've been known to travel as far as Europe if there's an auction with antique weapons that look interesting. Hell, I've got the money to spend, so why not?"

"No heirs to leave it all to? What about your wife?"

"She's got her own money. She inherited that from her dad, and with the investments he made it'll never run out. I got his practice and that was it, but that worked out all right for me once I got the hang of the back room deal." He paused and thoughtfully sipped his bourbon. "As for kids, it's the usual story. There's my daughter, Fiona, who's turned out gay and doesn't want anything to do with her 'corrupt' lawyer father. Like mother, like daughter – something about nuts not falling far from the tree. She's involved with a radical political theatre group here in Raleigh. Then there's my son, Victor the Petty Criminal. He's into guns, too, but not collecting them like me. He likes to point them at people to get the stuff in their pockets. I think he's dealing dope on the street, but I'm not sure 'bout that. I may be a success as an attorney, but as a father? Well... that's a whole other world of hurt."

That was a shocker. The surface of the sea may be smooth, but there are sometimes roiling currents and mobs of hungry sharks beneath. Arrington was an interesting mix of plusses and minuses, of "well done" and "look out for that falling anvil."

"I... er... I don't know how to respond to that," I mumbled. I gulped down some bourbon, emptying my glass.

"It's not your problem," Arrington said with determination and some vehemence. "It's my own doing and I have to live with it. You try to do the right thing, but with kids it's a crap shoot. Nature? Nurture? Who the hell knows?" he slurred.

"Where is he, your son?"

"Oh, he's around somewhere. I never know where until he hollers for help. He leaves for a while and then returns to the roost to hide out or recover from his wounds. He eats everything in the house, tries to get Simmy to give him the key to the collection, which she's under strict orders not to give him – though you can get it – he takes whatever cash he can find or something to hock, and then he's off on another round of craziness. At least he's not on drugs, I think. He's just a small time thief."

Arrington held up his empty whiskey glass. "You want any more?

"No, I'm good." To tell the truth, I was quite a bit more than merely good. I was pretty well snookered.

"Well, I'm done for tonight. Got to be relatively sharp for court tomorrow, even though everything's already been decided. The opposition tries to pull a last minute gambit sometimes. The judges aren't fools though; they've seen it all before and won't let any of us get away with anything... pretty much anyway. I should be home by one."

He rose, grabbed the arm of his chair to support himself and wandered unsteadily out of the room.

I followed. It had been an eventful day. Too much booze though. I'd have to watch myself on this trip. Arrington was no help in that regard. At least he was buying.

1838 Salerno, Italy

Two Duels in Three Days

Alfonso's wife had died in childbirth during his absence from Salerno, but she left him a perfect pair of twin sons. Carlo Davidi was the first by minutes. The second to emerge was named Armond Davidi. They would carry on the family and its traditions. A wet nurse had been found for them and the boys were doing well.

Alfonso studied the twin cribs that held his sons. "You are my cherubs, but the world you have entered is fraught with dangers personal as well as political. I'll do my best to protect you, but it's the nature of the times – and not much different from any other time in human history and probably its future. We are the creatures we are, not better certainly, and perhaps a bit worse."

His grief was deep, but Alfonso knew what had to be done. He hardened his heart to the task before him.

Alfonso had given hard thought to launching his vendetta against Lieutenant Romano. He argued with his father. Should Alfonso meet Romano in a fair fight? Father and son stood over the open box containing the matched pistols. The beauty of them as objects d'art belied their ingenious murderous design and intent.

Alfonso planned to find the lieutenant and kill him, not in ambush, but perhaps without the strict formalities of a duel. "The man has no honor and should die in the gutter. To take advantage of Stefano's youth and kill an inexperienced boy like that… for what? To cut another notch into his sword hilt?"

"But think of our family's honor," his father countered. "We have lived here for generations and are known to everyone. A fair fight to right a wrong is the only honorable way. Anything else would brand you a murderer. We would have to leave Italy."

"I am determined to avenge Stefano's death. I will kill the man, fairly or not. He will not do any more damage to the innocent. I swear it."

Since returning to Salerno. Alfonso had mourned his recently deceased wife. He was oppressed by the loss of his long-time companion.

One clear and warm day, he went for a walk thinking that a drink would be a nice way to kill some time. The alcohol might help to lighten his black mood. Serendipity intervened and unexpectedly broadened his options. His plan suddenly changed when he spotted Lieutenant Romano and several companions at a sidewalk café.

Briskly walking to their table, he snatched the drink from the killer's hand and threw the contents into the man's face.

"I'll kill you for that," the enraged lieutenant barked as he sprang to his feet.

"I doubt it." Alfonso countered. "You killed my brother Stefano Davidi, and now it's your turn to die."

The lieutenant blustered, but quickly got control of himself. "Swords or pistols? I give you the chance to decide how you will die. Choose."

"It's pistols then. I have recently acquired a set of duelers from Paris. They have proven to be accurate when killing rabbits in the field. You will be my next rabbit."

The remark enflamed the lieutenant even more. "A rabbit! Indeed! This is intolerable! Tomorrow morning, at the Castello," he roared.

Alfonso bowed graciously and sauntered off smiling. An appointment with destiny had been set.

Dawn comes in many flavors. It can seem sudden, when a clear sky of blue is brilliantly lit by a blaze of sunlight. It can come slowly as the full range of colors crosses the sky's palette from deepest black through pinks, reds and oranges to full daylight. On this cool and colorless day a man would die. The blue sky above was hidden by billows of dark gray clouds, clouds which reached beyond the range of human sight, perhaps all the way to the stars. The clouds bumped and jostled, actively seeking the best view of the death below where two humans would battle for... for what? The clouds would never understand human motivations. It's difficult enough for humans to understand.

Lieutenant Romano appeared in full dress uniform with his doctor and Bellitro, his regular second, in tow. He was as ready as he could be, having practiced the previous afternoon with his own dueling pistols. He wondered why he had accepted the use of the upstart Alfonso's guns, but it didn't matter. He would prevail regardless. A gun was a gun, was it not? One bullet could be as fatal as another. This affair was an irritant; he was hungry and wanted to go to breakfast.

As day brightened to its maximum dimness, Alfonso arrived with his second, Antonio Ravelli. Ravelli hadn't wanted to attend. He had known the boys for years and was afraid he would see Alfonso murdered like his younger brother, the family finally destroyed by the lieutenant's bullet. But he knew his duty, and trudged up the hill to the traditional local dueling ground with the walnut box containing Prélat's magnificent pistols. What difference did it make whether one was killed by a work of art or a work of pure utility like the plain, undecorated English pistols that were the vogue?

The seconds met on neutral ground off to one side. There, in the presence of themselves and the lieutenant's doctor, they loaded the pistols: powder, wad, the .38 caliber balls, tamping it all home with the same number of rammer plunges, carefully placing the percussion caps on the nipples in front of the barrel tang. The weapons ready, they were again laid in the box and the box was presented to Alfonso to make the first choice.

The guns were the same. They were precision instruments and Alfonso had complete faith in their lock mechanisms. They would not fail. The loads were the same and fresh. It didn't matter which pistol he chose. He lifted one from the case and hefted the gun. It felt familiar, a friend in adversity. One man sought revenge.

To the other, this was almost a game. He planned to kill his man and then meet friends for a meal as he had at other times.

Bellitro had started the duel which killed Stefano. It had been agreed that Ravelli would give the signal to fire this time. They would shoot up to three rounds. If no one was hit, the matter would be considered resolved. But of course, the goal in these matters was for someone to be hit, usually seriously, preferably fatally.

The seconds paced off twenty paces and marked the two spots. Alfonso walked to his designated firing position. The lieutenant did the same in a most military manner. The principals faced one another, then turned sideways to present the narrowest possible target.

Ravelli said, "I shall count to three, then say 'fire,' at which time you are free to shoot. Gentlemen, are you ready?" Both men acknowledged their readiness and Ravelli began his count. "One… two… three…fire."

Alfonso's rabbit shooting served him well. The explosion of black powder in Alfonso's gun barrel sent his bullet before the lieutenant's gun was properly raised to firing position and aimed. The bullet hit the lieutenant in the head and he dropped to the ground. It was over. A clean kill.

Bellitro went to his downed man and picked up the unfired Prélat pistol. It had to be checked. If it had been tampered with, the lieutenant's demise would be considered murder instead of a legitimate dueling death. He pointed the pistol at the ground and pulled the trigger. Bang! There had been nothing wrong with the gun or the load. Alfonso had simply been quicker, and his shot had been accurate.

Ravelli took the pistol from Bellitro's hand and placed it back in its case. He grabbed Alfonso by the arm. "Those shots will have been heard. We need to leave here now. The authorities will be here shortly."

Dueling was still illegal, but there were many sword and pistol enthusiasts about. The polizia would arrest anyone they thought involved. There might or might not be a prosecution for murder. It sometimes depended on how much the judge had been paid. The judge might have argued with his wife and was in a bad mood. Court results were unpredictable.

Alfonso and Ravelli left the dueling ground.

An eye for an eye, a death for a death. Balance had been restored. Nothing would bring Stefano back to life, but his death had been avenged.

It didn't take long for news of the lieutenant's death to spread. Salerno, though a center of education, culture and relative sophistication, wasn't a very large town. Many people felt relief that the lieutenant was dead. Self confidence was one thing, but bullying arrogance was altogether different. He wouldn't be ordering people around any more. He wouldn't be missed by those he'd harassed.

Old friends congratulated Alfonso on his triumph, but Alfonso wasn't proud of it. The death had occurred in a duel, a fair fight with matched pistols, but it could have gone the other way just as easily if the lieutenant had been a bit quicker.

Within the week, Bellitro appeared at Alfonso's home with two other soldiers from the lieutenant's regiment.

"I am here to right a grievous wrong. You killed my friend Romano," he said without preamble.

"He killed my brother. I only did what was right for my family," Alfonso answered. "I have no quarrel with you."

"Perhaps you don't, but I have a score to settle with you for the loss of my friend. I call you out." Bellitro persisted.

Alfonso sighed. Bellitro had clearly come to pick a fight. Challenged, Alfonso had the choice of weapons. "All right then. It's pistols again. You have already handled them. Tomorrow, on the usual ground, at the Castello."

It didn't matter whether Bellitro had practiced. Alfonso wasn't looking forward to the "interview," as duels were sometimes euphemistically called. He expected to be the victor and not the vanquished. He had practiced with his guns and was ready. But…

The night before the duel, the stars and moon were obscured by broken cloud cover that came and went. When the clouds came, they brought a cold drizzling rain with them. This was a danger for a pistol duel. In earlier times, only a few years before, all pistols were flintlocks. Because of the design of their firing mechanisms, wet weather could dampen the black powder in the primer pan and prevent firing. Alfonso hadn't fired his guns in this sort of weather, so he didn't know if they would fire or not, but these were of the newer style and their percussion cap ignition system promised a better chance of ignition. That was why the percussion system had been designed.

The following morning, the weather hadn't improved. The sky lightened then darkened alternately as moisture-laden clouds blew over the town from the Mediterranean. To be sure of prevailing in all eventualities, Alfonso armed himself with a short-sword that hung from his belt and a stiletto tucked down into his boot, the assassin's traditional 10-inch *arma insidiosa*. Whatever the weather, this problem would end today.

Ravelli slept at Alfonso's that night so they would be up and away early as the sky began to lighten. Before they left the house, Alfonso stood looking at his sleeping twin boys. "I am off to finally settle the business of your uncle Stefano's murder. It is a matter of family honor. I hope you will never have to face the same dilemma. Be good, my sons, and seek peace, but always remember the family's honor."

Arriving at the Castello, they found an angry Bellitro waiting for them with two uniformed companions from Lieutenant Romano's regiment.

"Have you made your peace with God, Davidi?"

"And you, Bellitro? Have you spoken to the Devil about your accommodations?"

Ravelli stepped between the antagonists. "*The Code* demands that you shall not speak to one another. It is for us seconds to make the arrangements. Step away from each other."

The antagonists did, though their glares seemed to light up the ground between them. It was just the sun trying to peek through the clouds, then disappearing fully again in the drizzle.

The seconds conferred. It was decided: 12 paces and the order to fire was "fire, one, two, three," both men to fire on three. If necessary, a second and then third round of fire would follow. Alfonso knew he wouldn't need three rounds.

The seconds loaded the paired Prélat pistols carefully. They measured the powder, rammed it, the wads and the .38-caliber balls home. Gently, they cocked the pieces.

The belligerents took their positions at 12 paces. There, the seconds handed a pistol each to Alfonso and Bellitro. Bellitro hefted his to get the weight and balance of the gun. He was ready for whatever came. He had come to kill this Davidi dog.

"Gentlemen, are you ready?" asked Ravelli. An affirmative answer came from each man.

A song bird trilled in a tree above the dueling ground. A distant dog barked.

Ravelli continued the ritual litany with "Fire... one... two... three."

A single roaring blast was heard as the two men fired simultaneously.

Crows and songbirds alike were disturbed by the roar and flew away squawking. A single black wing feather fluttered down behind them.

Bellitro and Alfonso stood still in frozen postures looking at one another. A trickle of blood ran weakly down Alfonso's left arm and puddled on the paving stones.

Bellitro, a stunned look on his face, muttered, "You have killed me, Davidi. Damn you." And with those anguished words, he collapsed to the sodden ground, the .38-caliber leaden ball in his heart having the final word.

Ravelli ran to see to Alfonso's wound.

Alfonso shook him off. "It's nothing. Just a scratch. Get the guns and let's be gone. The shots will bring the polizia as usual."

Ravelli ran from Alfonso to the fallen Bellitro. He snatched up the Prélat pistol, dropped it back into the case with its mate and the two men left the Castello grounds as fast as they could by a little-used lovers' path. They could hear boots running up the main Castello approach road. The polizia were awake and alert that morning, unlike their normally languid hung-over selves.

The district polizia chief and several of his minions stopped at Alfonso's home that evening.

"Where is he, your son, the murderer Alfonso Davidi?" demanded the sergeant.

"He left early this morning," his father answered. "I haven't seen him today."

"He'd better not return. We'll have his head on a pike if he does. He's killed two men now."

When the polizia had left, Alfonso came up from the cellar.

Father and son looked at one another. It was time for a major family decision.

"When will you leave?" the father asked.

"As soon as possible. Tomorrow or the next day. There is too much to remember here," Alfonso responded. "When I am established in London, I will send for you and the twins. Until then I leave them here in your care."

"Don't worry. I will take the very best care of them. They are of my blood, too."

Stefano was dead and his other son Alfonso was leaving for life in another country. Sadness swept over the father, but he would have the twins, at least for a while. And when Alfonso called for them, he would take them to England himself.

And so it happened that Alfonso Davidi, recent graduate in chemistry and medicine from the University of Salerno, would make his way to a new country. When he was ready and felt secure, the family would be reunited and all share in Alfonso's new, and hopefully better, life.

Wednesday

The Morning After

I awoke at 6:30 with a slight headache, as I had on so many other days. *Alcohol will undoubtedly be my downfall,* I thought yet again. Arrington could hold his liquor, perhaps because of his greater body mass, but I wasn't all that hefty, especially being as out of shape as I generally am. Alcohol went to my head and stayed there. At least I didn't awaken still drunk. That's when I hate myself the most. My problem then was too immediate to ignore or rationalize away.

What woke me that morning was the slamming of a door. I assumed it was Arrington leaving for his office. I got up, and after some perfunctory ablutions, sat down at the little writing desk by the front window and looked at my laptop. I didn't particularly feel like doing any concentrated thinking, but it takes discipline to be a pro. And a pro is what I'm supposed to be. Occasionally, I have to prove it to myself, if not to others. This was one of those days.

First things first. I opened my genealogy program, started a file, and entered the names and dates I knew: the Arrington nuclear family. I had to laugh. From what Wally had told me the previous evening, that phrase sure fit this little group of explosive personalities.

The people in this mildly radioactive bunch were Wallace Arrington and his wife Celine Arley Arrington, their estranged thespian daughter Fiona, and their black sheep son, Victor, the purported thief. What made this group different from any other family? As Tolstoy said in *Anna Karenina,* "Happy families are all alike; every unhappy family is unhappy in its own way." From what I'd heard so far, this wasn't much of a family at all. The two

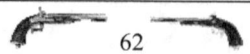

principals were related by a long ago business marriage, and two others by accidents of being born to the two related by marriage. Other than that, the four of them seemed to be uninvolved with one another and to live totally separate lives.

Oh, well. It wasn't up to me to pass judgment on anyone or any group. All I needed to do was hunt for historical facts and pull them together into a tapestry of relationships over time. I was seeking an object. The relationships that hid that object from view only interested me for how they affected the object. My opinions, of which I have many, and more all the time, didn't matter at all.

My broadly sketched plan was to track the family connections backwards in time until I found the point where the family split, then follow the other branch forward until I located the sought-for artifact. Of course, this plan was based on the assumption that the gun was still somewhere in the family line. I was making the same assumption that Wally admitted to last night. It might be far off the mark, but at least it was a logical strategy to begin with. If the gun wasn't still held by the descendants, someone might know to whom it had been sold.

Genealogical investigations usually start in the present. Here, there are living people to interview about relationships, family animosities, business interests, various comings and goings legit and not so legit, and a great deal more. It was like being an interrogating cop. Oddly enough, people divulged things they would never say to one another, but it was no problem to tell a stranger. For the moment, that stranger was me. Much of what I got was family legend, usually accompanied by lots of colorful opinion, but sometimes they even told the truth. I had to verify what was true and find out why they held those particular opinions about each another.

I started with Celine Arley. She was the true-blooded Davidi. Who were her parents? We hadn't been introduced yet and there had been no opportunity to interview her about her family. I'd have to dig out the information on my own. Luckily, I am a skilled genealogical researcher: Ben Bones, Articulator of Family Skeletons. That's what it says on my business card. *Ok, Bones, prove it.*

It was time to check the census enumerations. Being that the 1940 census was the most recently released to the public, I logged onto https://1940census.archives.gov to search for Arleys in Wake County, North Carolina where Raleigh is located. Needless to say, there were several hundred census enumeration sheets to search through. I didn't plan on going blind squinting at my laptop screen searching through them all. A street address would help before going any farther, but there was no one in the house to ask. Maybe Simmy? I'd have to check with her later.

Perhaps a different tack: the phone directory for 1940. No good. The highly useful website http://ncgenweb.us/nc/wake/directories/ had disappeared since I'd last used it.

Maybe a business directory would do. I hit pay dirt in *Hill's Raleigh City Directory* for 1960 which I found in a few minutes at https://archive.org/details/hillsraleighwake1960hill. The Arleys were on page 21, both the law offices of Arley, Benton and Feingold and the home address of Adam and Alice Benton Arley. That was it! Exactly what I was after. I returned to the census and typed in the Benton home address. Besides being too clever sometimes, occasionally I'm lucky. The Bentons had lived at the same address in the 1940 census. I like stable people. They make my job so much easier.

Checking Wake County property records, I found a Deed of Trust for the Benton property in the names of Adam Arley and his wife Alice Davisson Benton Arley as grantees. Davisson? Was that close enough to Davidi to be a formal name change? And what about the name Benton? Who was that? Alice's dad? Sure enough.

It's always a problem tracing families through the women. They tend to change their names when they marry, and more recently, when they divorce. Why should this family be any different? More formal sorts may only add their husband's last name as an addendum to their maiden name. That's what Alice had done.

I was on a good track for these folks. Name changes not withstanding, I was beginning to see the chain going backwards in time. Wally Arrington had married Celine Arley and somewhere in

---

the process, he'd taken over the elder Arley's law practice. Adam Arley, Celine's father, was married to Alice Benton.

Rudolph Benton had shared a legal practice with Adam Arley, and in the 1930 census, I found Benton's little family group. There was the newly born Alice, all right, but the surprise was that Rudolph Benton was married to one Magdah Davisson. Davisson! That was the key name in this particular puzzle.

I took another step backward into the 1920 census and discovered that Magdah was the daughter of one Ballantine Davisson. According to the census, Ballantine worked as a law clerk, and a 25 year old Rudolph Benton and his 21 year old wife Magdah were living with them. Ballantine's father, Armond Davis, born in Salerno, Italy, was living with Ballantine as well, along with his wife, a woman born in Basingstoke, England, wherever that might be. I was sure I'd know before too long.

Ballantine was still the head of household in the 1910 census. He and his wife were both 38. His parents, Armond Davis and Bela Jenkins, 71 and 64 respectively, were living with them. That was it. I was close to the turning point, the point at which the family had come to the United States.

It was time to find out when and where Armond had entered the USA.

Those early census forms gathered all sorts of useful information. Key to what I wanted was the birthplace of Armond Davis, which was listed as Salerno, Italy. The 1900 census said he had immigrated to this country in 1871. That was easy enough to discover.

The 1890 census had largely been destroyed by overly officious and tidy government workers helped by a fire in the records. I tried searching the 1880 census index looking for Armond in Raleigh. I was lucky once again, or at least I was searching for a steady type of fellow.

Armond, 41 years old at the time, his 34 year old wife Bela Silkie Jenkins, and their 8 year old son Ballantine were living in Raleigh, North Carolina in 1880. He'd arrived here in 1871. From Salerno, Italy? Hmmm. He was married to a woman from Basingstoke in England. Where had they met? Where had they married? When had all that happened? It was time for me to hit the immigration and passenger arrival records before making an extended online junket to "Merry Olde England."

The work was easy and going smoothly. No heavy lifting. I might well be in the process of earning a fast ten grand.

I did mention the money, didn't I?

Simmy's Summons

There was a knock on the oaken bedroom door. Opening it, I was greeted by Arrington's paired Dobermans Guilt and Innocence, accompanied by the diminutive Simmy. I'm not the tallest man I know, but I towered over this misshapen old lady.

"Mr. Bones, I be serving breakfast downstairs if'n you want t'eat."

Her straight-forward factual message delivered, she turned and left, trailed by the guardian beasts. Simmy was a woman whose role was to serve, not to entertain.

I looked at my laptop on the table by the window. It should be safe there, I thought. But there was Victor to consider, even though I hadn't met him yet. He might be making a home visit and from what his father told me, he wasn't to be trusted. I copied the new Davidi genealogical file to my USB thumb drive, dropped it into my pocket, then unplugged the computer and placed it inconspicuously between the bedstead and the wall. Out of sight, out of mind. A paranoid's work is never done. Over the years I've found that a little paranoia sometimes goes a long way.

Breakfast was amazing, considering that I was the only one eating, in fact the only one sitting at the huge banquet table. Eggs any way I wanted them, pancakes, Canadian bacon, a thick slice of country ham, grits (if I wanted 'em, which I didn't), excellent coffee. She even offered to spike my coffee with some of Arrington's hooch if I'd asked for it. I expected to be staying in Arrington's digs only a few days, but I could imagine myself unable to squeeze in behind the wheel of my Honda when it was time to leave.

After stuffing myself with Simmy's delicious homemade country cooking, she brought two cups of coffee to the postprandial table and we chatted like old friends. It was an opportunity to probe into the family's history a bit. I was curious about this little old lady. According to the census enumeration sheets, she'd been with the family through several generations.

"Not to get personal, Simmy, but how old are you?"

At my question, a change came over wrinkled old crone; she suddenly straightened up some and seemed to grow younger, the manner and slow smile of the coquette taking over her features. I got the long answer. She angled her head to one side and shyly said, "Much longer than you can imagine. You jes' a young man. You ain't lived long enough yet to know all's I know and to've seen all's I've seen. In my life, I gone from driving a mule cart on a dirt track to landing on the moon in a rocket ship. I been on this good earth a while. Got a good long while yet to go, too."

"And how long have you worked for Mr. Arrington?"

"As long as he been married to Miss Celine. I came with her from Mr. Benton. Been with her since she was a baby."

"So you knew her parents, too?"

"I was with them for years before she been born. She was a only child, as people say. Miss Alice, Celine's mother that is, died fairly young, and Mr. Arley... well, he never got over that all together. He never married agin. I raised that girl like my own." She paused for breath and for memory to refresh. "An' I still be wit' her today."

"Her daddy was a lawyer. According to Mr. Arrington, he took over his father-in-law's practice when the old man retired."

"Mr. Arrington said that? Well, well. Y'know, I have a hard time with anything that man says." She gave me a sideways look and said, "And don't believe everything he tells you neither. I'm not saying he's a liar, but he can twist things, say one thing and mean something completely different. You won't find out until much later... sometimes too much later. The truth is, Mr. Arley was forced out of his lawyer bid'ness. There was some kind of fancy deal going on with the city and some bid'nessmen. The sun come up one mornin' an' Mr. Arley was retired and Wally Arrington was the boss."

"I'll keep all that in mind. It's interesting, but that's not why I came to Raleigh."

"I know. It's all about that gun that he's been looking for. It preys on his mind. Has done for years."

"Ain't that the truth," said a deep baritone voice from the doorway.

I looked up to see a sparsely bearded young man in scuffed cowboy boots, holed jeans, a too-tight black t-shirt and an oversized brown leather bomber jacket. His shaggy hair was brown on one side, blazing scarlet on top, blond and black streaked on the other side. I couldn't see the back.

"Mornin', Victa'," said Simmy in a bothered tone of voice. "You want something to eat? There's a mess o' breakfast leftovers. Mr. Bone' here ain't much of a eater." With that, she left the room for the kitchen.

So this was the infamous Victor, described by his very own father as a petty thief and overly unsuccessful ne'er-do-well. In spite of all the money in the family on both mother's and father's sides, he looked like he'd been living kinda rough.

I rose to my feet and put my hand out. "I'm Ben Bones, and I'm here to…"

Victor cut me off. "Yeah, yeah, I know all about it. You're supposed to find that damn gun he's been obsessed with for years. Good luck with that."

"Yes, that's right. He's trying to reunite the set."

"The guy's nuts, if you ask me. If all he was after was to put the two guns back together, why doesn't he just put his up for auction? Whoever has the other one might want to match 'em up again, too. At least he'd know where the other one was then."

"An interesting approach," I said. "Actually makes good sense. Let the sought after become the seeker." I leaned back in my chair. "I like that idea. But he wouldn't go for it. He wants to own the pair. It's the collector syndrome hard at work. I've seen it before."

Simmy arrived just then balancing a tray loaded with breakfast goodies. Victor eagerly dug in like a man who hadn't eaten in days. From the look of him, that might've been the case.

As Victor shoveled it all in, Simmy and I exchanged looks. I wasn't quite sure what her look was supposed to mean. Mine was a question. What exactly was going on here?

Victor finished his gorging with a cup of coffee to which he'd added several spoonfuls of sugar. He sat back and patted his stomach. "Wonderful. Simmy, you haven't lost your touch. That was great."

"You'd enjoy it more if'n ya' slowed down to taste it," Simmy said as she cleared his debris.

Victor snorted a laugh and turned to me. "She gives me the same line every time I eat her vittles. She's a great cook, ain't she? Been with the family since before I was born."

I agreed that she was an excellent cook. Victor wasn't quite done with me.

"Hey, Bones... that's your name, right? Can you loan me 20 bucks?" he hustled. "I'll get ole Wally to pay you back."

This guy was really something. A broke rich kid? Or was this a manipulation test to see how far he could get? Either way, he wasn't getting 20 bucks from me. I'd just met him, but I'd been forewarned.

Recognizing the reality of our relationship, Victor turned his attention back to other matters. "Simmy, gimme the key to the gun room."

"Yo' daddy said I shouldn't do that. You don't want me to get fired for disobeying his strict order. You'd starve to death."

He laughed but wheedled on. "Come on. He won't fire you. It's not like he don't know me. I'm part of the family."

"Tha's right. Part of the family and he know you on'y too well." She pointed a boney finger at him. "That's why you don't get no key." Shaking her finger at him, she added, "You know 'zackly what I be talkin' 'bout, too."

A Mother's Love

I'd like to say that Celine Arrington's arrival blew some fresh air into a situation that was rapidly going stale, but it was more like a tornado blowing a prairie town apart.

"Victor! What the hell are you doing here?"

Victor leaned his chair back on two legs.

"Hi, mom. I love you too, mom," he said with a nod of his multi-colored head and a facetious politician's false smile.

"Just finish your damn breakfast and get out of this house! Simmy, you know how to handle this, right? And smash the dishes he ate off of."

She was sharp in manner and equally sharp-featured, her face focused at the end of her pointy nose almost like a muzzle, short black hair combed straight back, eyebrows tweezed to questioning wisps, her red-lipped mouth like a puncture wound in her pure white facial mask. She was thin and angular throughout, only about 5 feet tall, but obviously a determined personal powerhouse.

Having been through this scenario before, Simmy calmly handed the missus a "go cup" of black coffee.

"Did you hear me, Victor? I want you out of here!"

Victor dropped his chair back on all four legs and slowly rose. "Yeah, yeah, I got it. You haven't changed. And neither have my family allegiances." He shuffled toward the door. "Hey, Bones. Twenty bucks? Ten bucks?"

I ignored his request.

"Get out of here!" his mother shrieked. "Get out!" Her coffee sloshed onto the table and flowed onto the tile floor.

Simmy grabbed the towel that hung from her apron and went for the little black flood.

"Okay, I'm going," Victor muttered as he meandered out of the room. He stuck his head back in around the door jamb and stuck his tongue out at his mother. A Victory?

Family Skeletons

Wally Arrington had related a family saga to me last night over drinks.

At the simplest level, the story he told and the adventure I'm now telling you is the story of two guns, but it's also the story of two brothers. As a genealogist, I've learned that a family history is a great deal more than the listing of factual information: the names and places, dates of birth, death and marriage. A genealogical history must be about the people involved, for that is the stuff of human lives and thus human interest. If this tale were only about the guns, I could use it for a term paper and no one would care a bit what it said. But people… how they react to one another and to their various situations… their loves and animosities… their goals, their successes and failures… that's what makes a story worth reading. Yes, there was a factual basis to the story of the separated brothers. I had to excavate backwards in time to find where the family had been split, learn why that happened, and discover the consequences of that schism that these Arleys and Arringtons were living with.

According to Wally Arrington, the story began in the mid-1800s in Salerno, Italy. He told me that there were twins way back then when the family was first divided by the Atlantic Ocean. One twin, the one who came to America, was Wally's wife Celine's direct lineal ancestor. He knew that much, but without any details.

The second twin had remained in England. The family was thus effectively split, but not only by geography. As in many families, the cataclysmic split between branches was caused by inheritances delineated in a father's last will.

Wally had heard rumors in the family about a will that had broken the family apart. Oddly enough, even though he was a lawyer himself, he'd never searched for it or tried to acquire a copy. The single fact he did know, and that only through vague family legend, was that a set of dueling pistols had been shared out to the twin boys. He had acquired one of the pistols through marriage into the Davidi clan via Celine, and it had occurred to him to reunite the set. Over time, that random thought had become an obsession. Now, with my help, he hoped to finally realize his goal. Arrington wasn't a hunter, so he didn't want the gun for hunting. He wasn't a shooter of any sort, targets or competition, nor was he out to have an old fashioned pistol duel with anyone to settle a score. Wallace Arrington was a collector, a man obsessed by an idea and driven by a drive to acquire.

Frankly, I was curious about his motives. Many people who hire my researching skills are looking to reunite long lost family branches. They were looking for people, not merely artifacts. Here was a man with the financial resources to accomplish whatever he wanted, and all he was looking for was a gun. Not any gun, mind you, but a particular gun of a set that had been in the family and, who knows… it might still be. Half of the set was. But where was the other gun? By the luck of the draw, it had fallen to me to find the unattached branch of the family, and beyond that and more importantly, to find the gun. Arrington didn't give a damn about the family or old animosities that might still fester somewhere in the surviving Davidi DNA. All he wanted was another toy.

A Bit of History

The two guns comprised a set of matched dueling pistols crafted by François Prélat, one of the golden period of dueling pistol making's top Parisian gun makers of the early-to-mid 1800s. According to Lawyer Arrington, the pistols were purchased by his wife's long ago great-something-grandfather Alfonso Davidi, a father who split the set between his twin boys in his will, presumably for fairness. But as happens so many times in life when we act on our best intentions, unexpected consequences follow, and echo down the years.

Before coming east to Raleigh from my Asheville apartment, I had gone online and done some cursory poking around to see what there was on this Prélat character. What kind of a maniac was he? It turned out that he was much more than simply legit.

Typing the gunsmith's name into the *Google* search engine produced a bevy of websites, but there wasn't much information. Most of the websites cited one another, not with additional information, but mostly by copying and pasting each other's content.

François Prélat was an inventor and gunsmith who, along with Swiss gunsmith Jean Samuel Pauly, is credited with inventing the first self-contained cartridge around 1810. The cartridge contained a primer, black powder, and a round bullet all in a single unit. It made reloading muzzle loading weapons faster and easier, and by doing so, it moved warfare incrementally closer toward the orchestrated mechanized slaughter that we know all too well today. Prélat was a master craftsman in metal and fine woods whose exquisitely crafted matched pistols were made for a single purpose: to maim or kill an opponent, preferably the latter.

In addition to the basic technical facts, there was also an address for the gunsmith's shop in Paris. I started the *Google Earth* program. I love this program and this particular search is a prime example of why. I copied the gunsmith's shop address into the search field and was immediately transported to a street grid of the Montmartre region of Paris. But that wasn't enough for me. Being a diligent researcher as well as a thorough-going geek, I wanted to dig deeper.

On the *Google* page there's a small orange man off to one side. All one has to do is drag him down into the displayed street grid to place yourself in a street level photographic view. I dragged my little orange guy in and found myself "standing" in the rue des Trois-Frères. Moving the homunculus along the street, I was able to stand facing #4, the building where the guns were actually made. This is truly the magic of the Internet. Cheap sightseeing in foreign lands; I love it.

My next Internet search was for dueling. Going through all the listed websites took me a couple of hours. The Hamilton-Burr duel was covered extensively, but there was lots of other interesting historical material as well. Dueling was no "flash in the pan" event; it went on for hundreds of years, perhaps since the beginning of higher consciousness in our primate ancestors. That phrase itself, "flash in the pan," is from dueling. It connotes a failure to ignite the main charge in a loaded flintlock gun.

Dueling between individuals has a long history, perhaps as long as humans as such have been on earth. It's in our nature. I imagine that the first duels were fought with clubs by shambling half-apes as depicted in Kubrick's film *2001* when the chimps' battle for the water hole. As our awareness and tool use evolved, we improved our weapons. Clubs became swords, and swords eventually were replaced by guns. But I'm getting ahead of myself.

Dueling in Europe was a holdover from earlier medieval practices, from the days of jousting and trial by combat, when duels were performed by armored knights in front of king and court to prove innocence or guilt, to separate right from wrong, to test the lie or prove an asserted truth, the theory being that God favored the victorious and truth would thus be shown. For many years only the nobility dueled, but the practice spread from Italy through Europe and into all levels of society.

Originating around swordplay, trial by combat became the way people defended their honor, whether personal or familial, or simply as a way to prove one's courage. Swords were carried by gentlemen, wielded with skill born of long practice at fencing academies. Duels were freely used to settle accounts and as a means of proving oneself and righting wrongs, real or imagined.

The formal duel of "honor" is reported to have arrived in England from Italy in the late 1500s. Queen Elizabeth I tried unsuccessfully to outlaw this bloody method of dispute resolution. The upper classes took to it, and the practice filtered down to the mass of humanity. There were always querulous people itching for a fight, and a fight is always easy enough to find.

Just as the weapons evolved, so did the formalities that had to be observed by all participants. Codes of dueling etiquette were written. The *Code Duello* was written about 1777 by a committee of Irish duelists. It formalized the ritual of attempted murder over matters of pride by specifying strict rules under which a challenge could be initiated and had to be carried out. Seconds were introduced to present the conditions of a challenge, to make administrative decisions, and to control the actual occasion of the conflict. They had the authority to negotiate settlements, and to even cut a duel off under certain conditions such as first blood being drawn.

Back in those good old days, people took themselves and their honor seriously. A slight, whether real or imagined, had to be addressed.

Gentleman A (or sometimes a gentlewoman) found him/herself crossed by another's words, actions, insinuation, etc. Gentleman A demands "satisfaction" to prove he was in the right and inappropriately wronged by Gentleman B. A process was thus set in motion, inexorable as gravity. Seconds were recruited, pistols borrowed or purchased or retrieved from locked cabinets, and time, date and location for the event were set.

Civilization crawls forward on its hands and knees, changing its emphasis and fashion along with changes in its available technology. As humans developed the science of ballistics, and as ignition systems and guns were improved, the handgun replaced the sword to become the preferred weapon for settling personal disagreements. It was seen as a matter of fairness since the practiced swordsman had a definite advantage against an unskilled bladesman. Guns were simply more egalitarian.

Gunsmiths crafted accurate weapons for the purpose of killing an opponent. The English masters, men such as Egg, Manton, Nock and Wogden, made weapons that were strictly utilitarian. They were generally undecorated, the barrels heavy and not rifled. At one point, Manton made barrels with "secret rifling," in which, though the rifling couldn't be seen when looking into the barrel, the breech end of the barrel was gently rifled just enough to spin the bullet for greater accuracy. Though frowned upon, at least it was done to both guns of a set so that the two shooters had the same secret advantage.

French gun makers such as Prélat, Lepage, Boutet, and Gastine-Renette took a different approach. Though their weapons were also technically perfect and accurate, they tended to be highly decorated, true works of high craft, as well as instruments of death.

Though my story begins with the weapons themselves, it is also a story about people. After all, it's the people who perceived the interpersonal problems, who made the guns, who agreed to meet on an approved killing ground to do whatever damage they could to one another. The duel to the death was alive and well for a long time. In modern times, dueling is illegal most everywhere, but bar fights are basically the same thing: man battling man to prove a point of some sort, usually insignificant to anyone but the combatants.

Times have changed. Wallace Arrington, from what little I knew of him, was a civilized man of our time, an attorney, a man of rules and proscriptions. His interest in guns was academic rather than serving a practical need for a functional weapon. In North Carolina, it would have been easy enough for him to buy an efficient, multi-shot modern gun if he really needed to kill someone. Or he could hire the job out for a few thousand dollars. Why take the chance of being hurt or implicating oneself?

But he had come to me, hungry little Benjamin S. Bones, self-proclaimed "Articulator of Family Skeletons," to help with his gun collecting by finding a specific gun. Hey, I can do this. It's a job of family research, that's all, right? And did I ever mention the money?

The Library Adventure

Back upstairs in my bedroom, I found my laptop safely where I'd left it behind the bedstead. Since it didn't matter where I hooked up to the Internet, the bedroom was as good a place as any. But instead of going online, I thought it might be better to have a close look at some of the materials down in the library. Maybe there were some family records I could peruse. Computer in one hand, yellow legal pad in the other, and with a mechanical pencil tucked behind my ear, I headed down to the library on the first floor.

The staircase at the end of the hall was daunting. Its graceful circular sweep from the floor above filled the open three story atrium creating a feeling of grandeur and spaciousness. I made my way down to the first floor and toward the library, passing the dining room on my way. Simmy was there cleaning up from our earlier feast. She was humming what sounded like a dirge and didn't seem to notice me.

A short way down the hall was the library, another large room, this one done up in an almost medieval style. Five gothic stained glass mullioned windows rose from the floor to above the head height of an average man. The morning sun shining through them threw colorful designs on the oriental carpets scattered about the floor. Dust motes swam randomly in the descending rays.

Between the windows, dark wooden bookcases occupied most of the wall space. And they were packed. There were a good number of old leather-bound volumes in one glass-fronted case, while other doorless cases held more modern works. A multi-drawer chart table stood alone in a corner, rolled maps and charts standing in a bin next to it, and a conference table dominated the center of the room. I set my laptop there and fired the little guy up.

Taking a break from the one-man, one-guitar blues I listen to much of the time, I cued up some Thelonious Monk tunage. There's something about that guy's music. I like his sense of humor. It reminded me of the same humorous quality I'd found in Erik Satie's *Gymnopédie* and *Etudes*. With everything set up to my liking, it was time to dig in for another serious internet research session.

Up popped the correct census page. I do love the Internet! It makes hunting people down so much easier than in the good old days when you had to physically drag your carcass to the courthouse and choke in clouds of aging dust that billowed from the huge old tomes. Those searches were tedious: line by line for names, addresses, birth, death and marriage certificates. Times change, sometimes even for the better.

First off, I went back online to the 1955 *Raleigh City Directory*. I found Adam Arley listed as an attorney, but there was a second business listing for the man as an antiques dealer. My best shot after that was to check the 1940 census to see who was in the family unit, their relationships, where they were born, and who their parents were.

The 1940 census showed a family group composed of Adam Arley, listed as Head of Household, with Alice Davisson Benton listed as Wife. Celine was there as daughter, and surprise, surprise… Simmy Whittington was there too, listed as a domestic. An interesting little group to this genealogical detective.

So Simmy had been with the family for a long time. I'd have to interview her at greater length. She undoubtedly knew many of the family's secrets.

Alice Benton was the Davisson descendant. I had already known that from the carefully selected family facts imparted to me by Wally over drinks. I say "carefully selected" because, knowing lawyers and their ways, I was certain he would consider what he said before uttering a word, and he wasn't going to indiscriminately spill the family beans. You rarely knew everything that a lawyer was thinking, but you could always be sure that it was more than he or she let you know, even if they were on your side.

My concentration on the little screen was interrupted by a knocking at one of the gothic windows. I looked over and saw the shadow of a person blocking the sunlight from the last window on the right. More knocking. Someone was either testing the strength of the window or was trying to get my attention. I went over and opened the lower panel.

It was Victor.

"Hey, Bones, give me a hand will you? Help me up." He reached his hand in to have me grab it and haul him inside. I didn't cooperate. I didn't want to have anything to do with this guy.

"Come on, Bones. Help me out here," he demanded.

"Forget it, Victor. I'm here to do a job of research, not to be your enabler. Solve your own problems." After seeing the obvious dysfunction in this well-to-do family, I wasn't about to get involved.

"Simmy!" Victor called out in a rather too loud stage whisper. "Simmy!"

Simmy rushed into the library. "I hears ya, Mr. Victor. You hush now." She carried a paper sack. Whatever was in it rattled like glass against glass. It sounded like lots of little things.

"You got my stuff?" Victor asked the diminutive woman.

"Yes, I got 'em right here." She handed the bag out through the window. Victor grabbed it and opened the top folds to expose a jumble of small glass vials with black plastic screw tops. There might have been 30 or 40 of them.

He pulled one out and holding it between his thumb and forefinger, he let the sun shine through it. The clear emerald liquid inside glistened like a jewel. "This might be your best work, Simmy," he said.

"That should take care of you for a few days, Mr. Victor," Simmy said.

"I'll be back after I get rid of these. You get busy making some more," he told her.

"I knows what t' do," she answered petulantly.

Were they in business together? Was that dope she'd given him? Some voodoo concoction from her youthful island influences?

"What is that stuff?" I asked.

Victor tossed the vial he'd been holding toward me. I reflexively grabbed it.

"This is Simmy's special magic juice. It'll cure just about anything. Change your luck with women and dice. And it's legal, too. She's real good with plants and all such as that," Victor explained. "I sell 'em and make us some off-the-books cash, know wadda mean?" He winked at me. "That one's on the house, Bones. For all your help."

I looked at Simmy for confirmation, denial, anything.

"My family always been knowing the old ways. My grams taught me like hers taught her."

I turned back toward the window but Victor was gone, him and the paper sack full of vials.

"Simmy..." I started.

She interrupted. "It ain't none of yo' affair, Mr. Bones, so jes' let it be. And it ain't illegal neither, so there's nothin' t' be done 'bout it." She turned and left the room. I imagined her returning to the kitchen where a huge cauldron of the green stuff burbled away Shakespearianly while she danced around scantily clad in the best mythical witchy fashion.

This job was getting weirder and weirder. It's not that I haven't gotten involved in strange jobs before. Every job comes with its own wrinkles, just as every family has their secrets and intrigues. But voodoo? This was way far out of my experience, and probably something I didn't want to know about, shouldn't know about. They had their stuff going on, and had obviously been doing it for a while. Who was I to judge? I shouldn't have said anything.

I sat back down, set Victor's vial of emerald green fluid on the table, and looked at my computer screen, but didn't register what was displayed there. I was thinking about what I knew of the Arrington clan. I'd seen the animosities between mother and son boiling over at breakfast. That was hot enough to cool anyone's ardor. I hadn't met the daughter Fiona yet. I was sure that would be a unique treat, and would add another thick overlay of angst onto the home situation.

Where was Wally Arrington in this? Emotionally disengaged husband, father of two errant children, successful lawyer about town tangled up in back room deals, gun collector, and who knows what else? The layers of the onion were peeling back one at a time, inexorably showing the true natures of the beasts within.

I've been a genealogist for some years now, and I have to say it's interesting work. I get to learn lots about history and research techniques, but what inevitably surfaces in every job I take on is human nature in all its varied expressions. I have seen some relationships that raised my spirits and made me think, against my cynical tendencies, that all is well with the world and those who live on this planet with me. But I've also seen the ghastly side of the human animal, the side controlled by greed, the grasping for more money, more power or control over others. Humans are a varied lot, and there's no telling about the true nature of individuals by what their public faces show. It's like the old "can't tell a book by its cover" maxim. Yes, siree. "Hope for the best; prepare for the worst." I love those old aphorisms. There are always kernels of wisdom and truth buried in them. It's enough to turn even a happy and satisfied man like me into a sour cynic.

It seemed I'd fallen into another den of madmen... and madwomen from the look of things. I decided then and there to do the job as best I could, finish as quickly as I could, get my money in cash if possible, and return home to Asheville where I knew the lay of the land. No hidden dragons waited for me there.

Going Once, Going Twice

By the time Wally Arrington arrived home after court at 1 P.M. on the dot as promised, I had tracked the Davissons of Raleigh back in time to Ballantine Gravier Davisson. Davisson. Not the more common Davidson, and not the ancestral Italian name of Davidi. Davisson was unique enough that the next steps backwards in time should have been easy. Of course, they weren't. The trail petered out.

Wally Arrington came directly to the library. If nothing else, he was punctual. He looked at me sitting there in a t-shirt and jeans, with no socks or shoes.

"You ready to go to the auction?" he asked with one eyebrow raised. "They'll be showing some old firearms today and you can get an idea of the value of these things."

"Does the value have anything to do with my research? I'm looking for people, not money." I turned my laptop around so he could see the screen. "Here. Take a look at what I've found."

He waved a dismissing hand. "That's not the point. I want you to understand the totality of what you're doing for me."

My stomach grumbled. "I haven't had lunch yet."

Another dismissing hand. "Don't worry. They'll have sandwich stuff and drinks laid out for attendees. It's a classy kind of auction house." He chortled to himself. It was a private joke, and it looked like I wasn't going to be allowed to understand it.

Half an hour later, we were being driven across town by Arrington's Man Friday driver/bodyguard Zig to Obregon-Meller Auctions. I don't think Zig had a last surname. I never heard it. Wally'd had me change into a golf shirt and a sport jacket of Victor's so I'd look a bit more professional than my worn jeans allowed. I was even wearing socks.

As we got out of the car, Wally told Zig to pick us up in an hour. We headed for a glass door in a brick façade, a door with an awning over it and a doorman in fancy livery on duty to open the portal. He did and we entered into a whole other world.

I'd never been to an auction before, so the only ideas I had about these sort of events were from James Bond films and TV shows I'd seen. They were probably all bogus because they were written to fit a plot. My best strategy would be to watch and emulate. Even better, I should keep my mouth tightly shut for fear of ending up owning something I didn't want and in big money debt for the privilege.

As we entered, a svelte mocha-skinned woman I guessed to be in her mid-thirties appeared from nowhere. She stepped neatly between Arrington & me and slid a warm arm into the crooks of our elbows, one of us on either side of her. The top of her head came up to my eye level, though the thick black hair piled atop her head gave the illusion of greater height.

"Mr. Arrington. I'm so happy to see you again, and so soon, too," she cooed in a melodious voice.

"Hello, Odile. It's nice to see you too, though I know you're only after my money."

She blushed, beautifully I might add, the blood in her cheeks livening her naturally tan skin just enough. Her gaze shifted to me, cool and assessing, as if I were going up on the block for auction. "And who is this attractive gentleman?" She had a soft South or Central American accent. Where could she have come from? Where did they grow women like her? I wanted to go live there.

"This is my good friend Benjamin Bones," he said casually. "Bones, I want you to meet Odile Obregon, one of the auction house owners. She's a beauty, don't you think?"

I was flummoxed. I'm not that adept with the ladies to begin with, so I stammered out some sort of a lame greeting. It was impossible to shake hands being trapped in her arms as we were. I felt the heat of her through the sport coat Wally had suggested I wear.

Here I go again, I thought.

My luck with women hasn't been the greatest. After my wife and unborn child were killed in that drive-by shooting, I shut down emotionally for a few years. How could I not? But after a while, my male nature began to assert itself again and I started dating occasionally. I've already alluded to the fact that I'm not any sexual or even social champion. Besides the emotional issues, I find that maintaining a relationship is too much work for me. I tend to be too involved in my genealogical research anyway. Not to mention how expensive women are, even the budget models. So my feeble attempts usually come to nothing.

And now here was this exquisite creature snuggling up to me. I noticed that she'd dropped Arrington's arm and only clutched mine. *Danger!* my inner squirrel cried out. *Beware!*

Arrington pulled me back to reality from my reverie. "Come on, moonbeam. Let's go look at the guns."

I tried to untangle myself from the woman, but she held on as if she were drowning. "I've got to go. Arrington..." I said feebly, pointing with my free hand to my employer.

She pouted. "But we have just met. We need time to get acquainted, yes?"

"Ab... absolutely," I stuttered. I was in trouble. "Let me go look at the guns he brought me here to see. Then I'll come looking for you. Okay?"

She reluctantly freed my arm. She reached up and touched my cheek. "You must come back to me. Promise?"

My cheek burned at the point of contact. "Yes," was all I could get out, and that in a hoarse whisper.

She produced a business card from somewhere and slipped it into my shirt pocket, reaching into my sport jacket to do so. An intimate gesture. "Be sure to call me sometime. For lunch perhaps? Or something else." Did she just wink at me?

"Yeah, sure. Definitely. Soon," I mumbled.

I slid my arm out of her gentle grasp and scurried to catch up with Arrington as he crossed the large open showroom. I looked back over my shoulder at Odile. She had returned to her "real" world and was already greeting other people as they entered the auction house. I noticed that she greeted them with handshakes.

Arrington had picked up a colorful, expensive looking auction catalog and was making his way from display to display amongst other prospective bidders, checking item numbers and the estimated bid ranges in the book as he went.

Having never been to an auction before, I was fascinated by the variety and quality of the items for sale. There was a case of old fiddles with and without cases modern and vintage, a 6-foot long wooden airplane propeller, glassware, glassware, and more glassware, colored and clear, Louis XIV furniture originals and reproductions, daguerreotypes and tintypes in paper envelopes and leather folders, ceramic beer mugs, a fearsome concrete gargoyle head, an empty hornet nest on a branch, several swords of various styles, oriental rugs, statuary ranging from tabletop icons to life-sized people and horses, quilts and rag rugs, silver tea services, fishing rods and a reed creel, even a crossbow. Without searching for it, I had found an elephants' graveyard of civilization.

People milled around the vast open floor space trying to find specific items from the catalog to make their personal inspections, while others like myself wandered randomly. I kept an eye on Arrington in case he hailed me over to him. He ignored me completely in favor of the catalog.

But that was to change.

I inspected the crowd. It seemed normal enough: men and women of varying ages and physiques, undoubtedly of varying economic levels as well. Some men were older, none younger than middle age except for the occasional child held by a parental hand or a babe in a stroller. Women of all types: tall, short, round, angular, heavily made-up or beautiful without a supplemental chemical layer, hair piled high in formal arrangements or hanging loose, blonds, brunettes, the occasional redhead. Clothing ranged from what looked like business attire to torn jeans and one young woman in a black jumpsuit. Most were intent on the merchandise on display; some examined the human parade as I was doing. This auction was as much a social event as a business activity.

Arrington raised his arm and waved to get my attention. Since I had been watching for his signal, I hustled over to where he was standing in front of a tall glass-walled display case. Arrayed inside on the glass shelves were several flintlock and percussion cap pistols of varied antiquity.

"This is the stuff, the real stuff. I have several examples of this level of the gunsmith's craft at home. Those old guys were artists as well as gunsmiths." He pointed toward one of the more fancy weapons. "Just look at that handiwork."

I looked. It was truly impressive. The carvings of birds and mammals on the wooden furniture of the gun was beautifully detailed, and the worked metal fittings were equally lovely. This piece was a work of art, not for the hunting of wild game. But it was also an instrument specifically designed to kill another human being at close range, though in as elegant a manner as humanly possible.

"The bidding on this one will start at $3,500. Who knows where it will end up? And it's not even a matched set, just a lone, orphaned gun," Arrington commented.

He pointed to a tweedy gentleman with a cane and a meticulously carved Van Dyke beard. "See that guy? He's a collector too, but he's not exactly competition for me. He's more like an investor. He buys and sells. But he knows his guns and their values. Name's Winkler, Julius Winkler. European, British I think, but he lives here in Raleigh."

A noise like a gunshot rang through the hall. The facing panel of the case in front of us blew apart into a million shards of glass. The case collapsed to the floor. A second shot. A scream. More screaming. A rush of people in no particular direction. A third shot. Pandemonium.

I grabbed Arrington's jacket by the collar and threw my weight to the tile floor dragging him with me. We hit hard. He whooshed as the air left his lungs, and he lay there gasping for a breath that wouldn't come. I was breathing hard myself, but from the excitement, not the exertion of the take-down. Adrenalin had taken care of that action. And there was plenty left over, too. I was shaking uncontrollably.

People were running everywhere. There was no order to it. I wanted to check on Odile, but thought it better to keep my head down. I didn't care to be shot. It wasn't in my life plan. I'd managed to avoid it until now, not that my life hasn't been a tricky adventure at times. But I wasn't much of a risk taker, and I was determined to prove that once again.

There was another shot, then a flurry of pops in answer. I stuck my head up a bit and saw the auction's only uniformed guard in a shooting stance by the door, his service revolver held out in front of him with both hands, a terrified expression on his face as he pulled the trigger again and again until the gun was empty and then afterwards. But that scenario didn't last long.

There was another fusillade of shots from somewhere amongst the displays. The guard's head exploded in a shower of blood, brains, and bone. His lifeless body crumpled to the floor. A ninja in a black coverall leaped over the guard's corpse and ran out through the door followed by a crowd of panicky auction-goers. They didn't seem to notice they were following the attacker.

The auction was over for the day.

But the day wasn't over.

EMTs showed up within minutes followed by a bevy of cops in black riot gear and body armor waving their Heckler & Koch MP5 submachine guns in all directions. Odile and a tall, thin, bald man, gingerly avoiding the bloody security guy's corpse, met them.

"Don't anyone move. Stay exactly where you are," a cop hollered.

"What happened here? Was anyone hurt? Killed?"

Didn't they see the guard at the questioner's feet?

"How many of them were there?"

"Did anyone get a look at his face?"

"Was it a man or a woman? White or black? Middle Eastern? Oriental?"

"Which way did they go?"

"What kind of weapon did he or she have?"

"How many shots were fired?"

It went on like that for what seemed like hours: question after question, all of them dumb and repetitive. But we didn't have many answers for the detectives.

The EMTs worked patching people up. They pulled slivers of glass from Arrington and myself. He had gotten the worst of it standing as he was directly in front of the display case. I had a few pieces that had stuck into me when we hit the shattered glass on the tile floor.

Several cops, an EMT and a guy in a rumpled suit hovered over the unmoving body of the door guard.

"You guys were lucky," the EMT working on Arrington said.

Arrington, instead of being a terrified victim, was raging mad. "Who the hell did that guy think he was?"

"You ever see him before today?" asked a new voice. A detective in a tailored pin-striped blue suit and a Bugs Bunny tie stepped up.

"I didn't even see him this time," bellowed Arrington.

The detective flashed his badge. "I'm Perez. This is my case." He looked at the wrecked display. "From what I've heard so far, it looks like whoever it was shot at you initially. His first bullet struck the case right in front of you."

Arrington pushed an EMT away and pointed at himself. "Me?"

Perez nodded. "Tell me... do you have any enemies? Is someone out to get you? Maybe someone with a grudge?"

"My name's Wallace Arrington. I'm a lawyer. Of course I have enemies, and lots of grudges too, everyone from the guy who accepted a lousy divorce settlement to those jokers who are always innocent but are proven guilty anyway. You're old enough to have been around, Perez. You know how it goes."

"Yeah, I know. Everyone hates lawyers and dentists. But this isn't the best way to solve a dispute, is it? It's rare that someone shoots a dentist. But a lawyer... well, that's different. Too many of you guys anyway. Who was it, Arrington? You must have some idea."

Arrington rolled his eyes.

Perez turned to me. "Who are you? What are you doing here?"

"I'm Ben Bones, and I'm visiting Raleigh for a few days doing some research for Mr. Arrington here."

"Where you from? And what kind of research?"

I handed my business card to Perez.

"Gen'ologist, eh? My sister's into all that stuff." He eyed me suspiciously. "You actually earn a living at this?"

"Sometimes. It's not a steady pay check. I can tell you that. But I pay my bills."

He waved my card at me. "What else you do for money?"

I pointed at my card in his hand.

"And you're working for Mr. Attorney here?" Perez pressed on.

"Just for a few days. He has some questions he needs answered. This is my first day on the job. I hope they aren't all like this."

"Hmm," grunted Perez. "Where you staying? I might have some questions for you later."

"He's staying at my place. I'm in the phone book," Arrington interjected. His face was a patchwork of small white sticking plasters covering the pinprick holes the glass had made. "This is a load of crap. Let's get out of here," he said to me.

"Not yet," said Perez. "I've got a few more questions for you."

"Hundreds probably. I know how you guys work. Hows about I see you later? I've got work to do."

"You're not to leave town, understand? You neither, Mr. Bones."

Arrington waved off the cop's instruction. We left. I didn't spot the exotic Odile on our way out. I hoped she was all right.

Post-Auctional Languor

Back at the house, Arrington poured us each a double of some high-priced bourbon that went down much too smoothly. It was the kind of brown liquor that wouldn't warn you off by scorching out your esophagus. It was like drinking velvet and something I could easily get used to. Luckily, I probably couldn't afford it anyway.

That's the big problem, the trouble with having well-heeled clients. Sure, they'll pay whatever you say they owe you, but they're impossible to keep up with trading drink for drink. It's simply too expensive for me. But then, I'm not looking for equality with them. Crass as it sounds, I just want their money. I mean, we live in a culture that demands that sort of an attitude from us. Those who don't have a mind oriented toward the raking in of cash tend to fare poorly. Down deep, I'm one of them. I don't like the cutthroat competitive attitudes of my contemporaries, but as I've said, our capitalist culture is based on greed and acquisition, and requires the same behavior from us all. So I'll raise a glass to Arrington's good health and drink his good hooch whenever it's offered, and I'd do the best research work I can for him. Our deal had already been made, so I didn't need to keep track of the hours I put in on this job. All I had to do was produce the result he wanted.

But getting shot at wasn't something I'd agreed to. I doubt Wally had any idea that he would be targeted by some crazy person. And now that I was his genealogical factotum, had I become a target, too? Could the shooting have anything to do with my search for the other gun? Who else might know about our little arrangement except ourselves? We'd signed our contract yesterday at his office, so anyone who knew would have to be someone close to him, either a worker or a family member.

Victor? According to Wally, Victor's only interest in daddy's gun collection was to sell off the pieces one by one so he could buy more dope and get high again. Definitely a goal with a close horizon. That guy wasn't planning for some vague far-off future.

My mind was ticking away. The cops weren't the only ones full of questions for Arrington. "Do you know of anyone who's in competition with you for the other Prélat? And how would they know that you've initiated another search for it?"

He poured himself another double and raised the bottle up to me in offer. I shook my head. I didn't need further clouding of my thought processes.

"Nah. No one is even aware of the Prélat I have, no one except a few other carefully chosen collectors."

"That's exactly what I'm asking about," I blurted. "Give me a list of names and contact info of those guys. We'll pass the list on to the police and let them chase the people down to see where they were at the time of the shooting."

Arrington snorted. "You really think that someone with the money to be a gun collector would do the dirty work himself? Ridiculous. A few of those guys have long-standing ties to OSS, the CIA and other covert organizations, mercenary groups, and even the Ku Klux Klan. The sound of a gunshot? The smell of gun powder? Forget it. That'd be alien territory to most of them. They're academics, for crying out loud."

"Academics, eh? Well, benign collector or not, someone took a very real shot at you. Or me. Maybe it was a random shot at Odile's auction business. She must've pissed a few people off in her time."

"Don't drag her into this. She's absolutely legit. I've had her checked out by pros."

"And 'legit' people aren't murdered sometimes? Or driven to murder themselves? Come on, Wally. Get real. You're a lawyer. You must've seen this side of the human animal before. Except for simple real estate deals, any case with opposing positions will have sizzling animosities buried in it."

He slugged down his second double, then poured himself a single. He reached over and poured me one too against my weak protestations, then topped both our glasses off with an additional couple of splashes. That would make at least six belts for him and four plus for me. Not so good for analyzing facts.

Or doing any more research this day. I decided to pack it in, go upstairs, lie down and watch the room spin for a while.

Thursday

The Morning After the Morning After

I awoke with yet another headache. You ask why?

It's not like it's an organic disease process that'll keep on cooking in my brain until all the synapses are fried. No, not at all.

It's entirely my own fault. It's an alcohol induced malady, an incremental self-destruction chipping away at my gray matter.

And this Arrington character isn't helping me at all. He keeps on pouring. He can afford gallons of the stuff. No pocket-sized airplane bottles for him. No siree, Bob. He's a serious drinker who can afford the best. Actually, I think it's more a brand snobbery issue than a quality of intoxicant thing. Past a certain alcohol concentration in the bloodstream, nothing matters, does it?

So it was another sluggish rising this morning. That Arrington. He was a good bit heavier than I am. He had that Shmoo-like attorney physique from sitting at a desk plotting and scheming. As a result, he could soak up a good deal more liquor than I could and his body was used to metabolizing it. I'd hate to be his liver.

With those thoughts in mind, I rolled myself to the edge of the bed and swung my feet to the cold tile floor. Sitting up, my head went in two directions: the physical part to the left, my self-awareness to the right. How was I supposed to think clearly enough to get this job done with him pouring the booze like he did? I had to get control of myself and my situation here. Dissipation was too heartily encouraged.

I felt a good deal better after a quick shower. Then it was time for breakfast. I pulled on my jeans and a polo shirt and headed downstairs to the dining room where Simmy had laid out a breakfast buffet.

Wally was already seated at the head of the table when I arrived, a plate of scrambled eggs and bacon in front of him. A woman I hadn't seen before sat to his left. Along with a good deal of make-up that looked like it had been laid on with a trowel, she wore a large floppy-brimmed hat the brim of which she kept swatting away from in front of her eyes. False eyelashes brushed her over-size rose-tinted glasses. I guessed her age to be somewhere between 45 and 65. It was difficult to see the real person through the camouflage of her paint job and clever disguise.

"I want you to meet a friend of mine, Bones." He gestured toward the woman beside him fighting with her fashionable hat. "This here's Portella DeNight. Remember I told you about her? She's a colleague of yours, a genealogist who's worked for me on some of my family law cases. I asked her to search out the Davisson clan for me, but she only found a couple of names. She works cheaper than you, too."

"If I remember correctly, you set the price for this job. Could it be that out-of-town talent is more believable than someone home-grown?" I quipped. "That was our deal, and your decision," I reminded him.

I turned toward the lady. "Nice to meet you, Ms... ah..."

"DeNight," she croaked in a Southern drawl. "Portella DeNight. Portella Elnora Bakkernon DeNight." Her voice was a gravelly grinding that seemed to catch in her throat. "I'm a gen'ologist, too. And I don't know why he had to bring you over from... where was it now?" She pushed the brim of her hat out of the way so it didn't block her view of me. The brim fell right back.

"Asheville, 'cesspool of sin' and the tattoo capital of North Carolina."

"Right. I remember now. Sometimes I need a little reminder." She picked up her fancy mimosa flute and waggled it in the air. "You got any more of that mimosa fixed up? I could use a little boost this morning."

Simmy appeared from nowhere with a glass pitcher and poured the glass full. Portella drained the glass and held it back up for a refill. Simmy obliged without a raised eyebrow or a word.

Where was I? This adventure was becoming more and more like Lewis Carroll's *Alice's Adventures in Wonderland.* The only thing missing from the situation was a white rabbit with a pocket watch.

Simmy brought me a plate already mounded with scrambled eggs, bacon and sausage. I was starving and dug right in without apology.

"I wondered if you might need some help and asked Portella to stop by. Maybe she can give you a hand and speed things up," Arrington said.

I gulped down a hunk of biscuit slathered with honey. "I've got everything in hand, Wally. Besides, I'm doing most of my work on the Internet. There's only room for one at the keyboard."

Portella huffed and jerked herself up out of her chair. "Well, if that's the way you're going to be." She drained her mimosa glass, slammed the glass down on the table, an action which broke the stem, and headed unsteadily out the door, bumping into Victor as she exited.

Victor spun around and watched her go. "Sheesh! What's her problem? Dad, you've got some real weird friends. You know that, don't cha'?"

Wally was reaching for his wallet. "How much? How much you want this time? Gonna buy you some more dope?"

"Fifty dollars will do. You got small bills?"

Arrington handed the boy a 50-dollar bill. "It'll spend anyway you get it. You looking for a job these days? Or are you still bumming around town ruining the Arrington reputation?"

Victor folded the bill in half carefully and put it into his shirt pocket. That done, he snatched a sausage link off of Simmy's buffet tray and held it between thumb and forefinger like a cigar. Winking at me, he tapped off an imaginary ash, then stuffed the entire thing into his mouth. He turned toward me and spoke through a mouthful of half-masticated sausage.

"So how's it goin', Bones? You found my daddy's pistol yet?"

"Not yet, Victor, but I'm working on it."

Victor turned his full attention to loading a plate from the buffet and digging into it. He seemed to have few questions that needed to be solved in his life. Free food cooked by Simmy, a bit of cash in his pocket, no job to worry about being fired from… he had little enough to worry about.

Since my appetite was satisfied and the company was becoming irritating, I pushed away from the table and stood.

"I'll be in the library if you need me," I said to Wally.

"I'm headed for the office," Arrington said. "We'll talk when I get home. You'll have some good stuff for me, right?"

I nodded.

He pointed a finger at Victor. "This fellow here doesn't need to know anything, Bones. Don't tell him nothin', understand?"

"Yeah, sure. Whatever you say. You're the boss," I returned.

"That's 'xactly right, and don't anyone forget it," he said to everyone in the room. Victor snorted and Simmy rolled her eyes. They'd heard this pronouncement before.

I started for the door but stopped, a new thought emerging from my clearing brain. "Simmy, can you come to the library in a few minutes? I've got a few questions for you."

"Certainly, Mr. Bones. I be happy t' help y'all out."

Cops Come a'Calling

Back in the library, I turned my laptop on and hooked up with some blues piano from the post-war years in Chicago. Sunnyland Slim would do for this morning. With the blues for background, I reviewed what I had accomplished to date.

I had the skeleton of a family genealogy: Arrington's family as it had evolved in the U.S. of A.

I thought it strange that Arrington, who had married into the Davisson clan and had no blood relation, was the only one interested in the family history. But this wasn't the strangest thing I'd been called in on during my years as a genealogist. I'd searched for objects that weren't anywhere to be found, seen siblings kill one another off for money and property, found Poetry – a lost country town in rural Georgia – and uncovered crimes that included the rape of a slave woman, interstate bigamy, and murder most foul. Ah, the life of a genealogist… You'd think the worst thing that could happen would be a nasty paper cut, but I'd been shot at, chased and been the chaser, been run off the road, thrown into the ocean with hungry sharks, and even drugged to unconsciousness. As it turned out, my life as a genealogist was fraught with danger. Who could've guessed?

And now I was searching for an ancient dueling pistol that could be anywhere in the world: on display in a firearms museum, locked away in a Japanese collector's vault, or buried deep in a trash midden somewhere never to be seen again unless uncovered by archeologists 10,000 years hence.

Armond Davis had entered the country through the port of Philadelphia with his wife in tow in 1871. I knew that much. And I'd figured out how Armond was connected to Arrington down the years, but that was it. One leg of the search was done. There was no need to search for more details on the people I'd found. Since it was on the British side that I expected to find the gun, it was time to cross the pond and see what the family situation was in the United Kingdom.

My review was interrupted by a knuckle knocking on the door jamb. I looked up as Detective Perez entered the library.

"Morning, Mr. Bones. I'm Detective Perez."

"Yeah, I remember. It was only yesterday that we met."

"I've got a few questions for you. You got a minute?"

"Sure. I was just reviewing what I'd done so far for Arrington."

"That's one of my questions," Perez said as he stepped briskly toward the oak library table. "What exactly are you doing for Mr. Arrington? If it's not a breach of confidentiality to tell me, that is."

"Ordinarily it might be, but I don't see any harm in telling you. This is an official investigation, right? You're trying to find out why someone would take a shot at him... or whoever they were shooting at."

"That and other things. A guard was killed at the auction house yesterday. But that seems more like an unplanned act by a fleeing felon. I don't think the guard was the shooter's original target. The only other person shot at was Arrington. He was the first. Why would that be?"

"Bad luck? Being in the wrong place at the right time?" I speculated.

"Why are you here in Raleigh? You're a ways from home. Asheville, right?"

"You've got a good memory, Detective. I wish mine was as good."

Perez chuckled. "It's not really that great. Next week I'll have ten new cases and the facts of this one will have been pushed into my subconscious... unless a reminding clue surfaces. Then it all comes back in a rush."

I smiled. Perez seemed like an all right fellow. He was personable, polite, and professional. I decided to answer whatever he asked, within limits, of course. Most of my work is deemed to be confidential. That's part of the professional genealogist's code. But he was right; this was a murder investigation.

"Wally Arrington is a firearms collector. He's got a load of antique guns in a locked room in the basement here." I gestured toward the floor and the vault below. "But there's one gun that he's been seeking for years and hasn't been able to find. I'm here to help him find it."

Perez's brow furrowed at that. "How's a gen'alogist gonna find a missing gun? That don't make no sense."

"Actually, it does in this case. You see, he's got one gun of a set of matched dueling pistols, but the set was broken up years ago when the progenitor of the family died and gave one pistol to each of his two sons. Arrington, a collector who married into the line and isn't a blood relative by the way, wants to reunite the set, and he thinks that by tracking down the old man's descendants we'll find someone who owns the other pistol or knows where it went. When we find it, he plans to buy it from whomever. I was just about to start looking into the UK branch of the family, the folks who initially had the other pistol."

"Okay, now I get it. But that wouldn't make him a target, would it? I mean, who knows about the pistols and wants his half of the set enough to kill him for it?" He stopped and thought for a second. "Nah, too far-fetched. It's got to have been a disgruntled client or the loser in a law suit he handled. That's my theory. It makes lots more sense."

"I agree. You're probably right. But why take a shot at him in such a public place as the auction? Wouldn't it be better to find your victim alone somewhere and do the job privately?"

Perez nodded and rubbed his chin. "Actually, I think that's the only thing I needed to ask you. You've justified your presence here."

"I'll be around for another day or so. If you think of anything else, you can find me here. Or call my mobile." I whipped out one of my business cards and handed it to him with a flourish.

"Articulator of Family Skeletons," he read. "Clever. Okay, I'll be in touch." He turned to leave but pulled up short. "Say, I'm something of a firearms enthusiast myself. How can I get a look at his collection?"

"Arrington would be the first person to ask. Then you'd have to talk to the housekeeper Simmy. She's got the key."

"Okay. That's it for now. Thanks, Bones."

"No problem. Any time at all." And I meant it, too. Befriended cops have been a big help to me on other cases I've handled.

British Cousins

After Perez left, it took me a few minutes to reorient to my task. I felt good about our interaction. I hadn't been asked about anything I considered confidential, so I needn't have worried about breaching the code. And I had helped a cop out. That was always a good thing. It never hurts to have a friendly cop on your side. Positive interactions with cops on past cases have always worked out to the benefit of us both.

I didn't know where to begin with the British research. Until now, I'd done all of my research on this case using domestic USA material. Most of my work in the past had been on people in United States' records. This would be the first time I had to do an in-depth search in another country. At least they spoke English and not Croatian or Pashto. I'd be able to read any documents I located, if I could find them in the first place.

I had Armond Davis. And I knew he came to America in 1871 with a Prélat pistol in his luggage. But why had he come here? Why had he left the land where he'd grown up and whose customs and laws he knew? Was it just the search for a better life in a new land? Or had something chased him from the old country? How could I possibly figure out the motives of man who'd lived more than 100 years before me? It was a guessing game, and I was the guessee… or was I the guessor? I can never figure those word endings out and know who is what to whom. Lawyers!

I decided to go searching for a British census. Ours fell on the decade year, but theirs were one year later: 1881, 1891, etc. And I had no clue where to begin.

Wait a minute. Armond's wife Bela had been born in Basingstoke, wherever that was. It said so in the US census. I took a chance. I called up Google Earth and carefully typed in the town name: Basingstoke. Bang, there it was, to the west southwest of London, not too far north of the Isle of Wight, and in the county of Hampshire. That was easy enough. Now what?

Maybe a census? Maybe a town directory? Did Basingstoke even have a directory? And for what year? 1871 would be good, that being the year that Armond left England. I'd have to go back a bit further to see if they were there at all.

Something had caused his uprooting about that time. But why? Many people left old Europe during the late 1800s and the early Twentieth Century. They were impelled to leave Europe for all sorts of reasons and brought their skills and knowledge across the ocean and built America. Sometimes it was political. Was there a war he didn't support, complete with forced conscription?

Sometimes it was economics; did he have debts he couldn't pay? It could have been anything. Bastard children to support? A dispute with a potent foe such as a beaten business rival or an angry cuckolded husband? A dream of better prospects in the New World? At this point, all I knew was that he'd skedaddled with his wife, left the country and went off to find an altogether new life on the booming American frontier. Where were the clues hiding?

I leaned back in the heavy wooden library chair. What was really going on with this job? I was in Raleigh supposedly looking for a missing gun, but was there another agenda that was being kept hidden from me?

Arrington was a lawyer, and lawyers are known to have a fascinating array of tricks. A lawyer knows how to obfuscate, to cloud the issues, to emphasize the insignificant or avoid critical elements. What was hidden in his deeper thought levels? Was there an element of vendetta here? It didn't look like it. There was a family problem that no one had shown any interest in until now. Suddenly…

Arrington was a successful lawyer by the look of things. As such, he was loved by some and reviled by others. Had there been any threats? It doesn't matter how "clean" a life an attorney tries to lead; there will always be losers on one side of a case and winners on the other. Inevitably, someone is bound to feel they've been treated unfairly by an unscrupulous and corrupt legal system. Judges are accused of taking bribes, whether they do or don't, and lawyers of being the ones to deliver envelopes packed with $100 bills to obtain favorable verdicts for their clients or weaken the other side of a dispute.

How much of that is true? Probably very little. Judicial corruption continues to be a favorite topic for the muckrakers, but it's rarely the innocent folks who make the headlines.

What was really going on under the surface of my search? Who was what to whom? Who had a grudge? Who had what to gain? Who had what to lose?

The gun itself could be a dodge, a stated goal that actually was of no consequence, a convenient excuse to call in an expert to find... what? The gun? Or something far more important to the principals? Was I the victim of a complex manipulation by a treacherous and devious legal mind? I didn't know. If I were a bit more paranoid, I might believe that the job had suddenly taken on a seriously more sinister aspect. I simply didn't know.

I like to say jokingly that the life of a genealogist is fraught with danger. In the present situation, maybe that wasn't so funny after all. Hell, we'd been shot at.

My eyes were crossing from studying the little screen. My back was stiff and my stomach rumbled with hunger, or was it nerves? Sitting back in my chair, I looked at my watch. It was just about time for lunch and a good time for a break.

I hadn't been bothered by Victor this morning. He'd probably left the house after having a sumptuous Simmy breakfast and hustling his dad. I could leave my laptop here in the library without fear of its disappearing, but my basic paranoia warned me otherwise.

I copied the research and the genealogical chart that I'd built to a USB thumb drive and dropped it into my pocket. If anything happened to the computer, at least I'd have my data.

I unplugged the computer and put it on a high library shelf where it might be mistaken for a book on casual inspection. I left the house and headed out into the street...

...where I immediately bumped into a hurrying young woman, knocking her to the ground.

"Oh, I'm sorry. I wasn't paying attention. Are you all right?" I put my hand out to help her up.

"Right as I can be after that bumping you gave me," a British accent said to me. She avoided my hand and athletically sprang to her feet on her own.

"You're not from around here," I said, stating the obvious.

"How'd you guess, mate? Must 'a been something I said," she spat out. She dusted off the jeans and bomber jacket she wore.

"I'm just visiting Raleigh myself. For a few days. I'm doing some work for a guy," I explained. "Genealogy stuff. That's what I do. I'm a genealogist."

"That's just fascinating," she said, her red-rimmed mouth twisting up on one side. Her dark eyes flashed a deadly glare at me, then softened to a less hostile viewing.

Her skin was peachy colored, the dark eyes spaced pleasingly on either side of her sharply pointed nose. Her chin was sharp too, coming to a point below a distinct delineating cleft. Her dark hair was stick straight and blunt cut just above her shoulders. Very pleasant to look at, if it weren't for the onboard hostility. She was angry, and I couldn't blame her much. It was somehow a familiar look, though I couldn't possibly have seen her before.

"I... er..." My natural tendency to being tongue-tied in the presence of beauty asserted itself. "I mean... I'm Ben Bones. I'm a genealogist."

"Do you always repeat yourself? Must be hard on the people you deal with," she said. "You know... boring."

"Sorry. I'm just naturally nervous with women," I blurted.

"Well, you needn't be nervous with me," she said. "I'm out of 'ere." And with that she disengaged and headed down the street the way she'd been going when I crashed into her.

"Wait. What's your name?"

She whirled around and headed back toward me, her anger evident. "It's Carla, but what's that to you, mate? You think you're a ladies man, a rogue with the girls? You knock me on my bum and then ask me out? That's some technique you got there. Somethin' a bit different, I'll say. Well, don't bother."

With that said, she turned abruptly and continued on her way. I watched her go.

At the corner, she stopped and waved a greeting to someone. A man approached her, a man with multi-colored hair. Victor. They chatted for a minute with no hostility evident. Their hands came together for an instant and I thought I saw a flash of emerald green in the sunlight, after which they went their separate ways. Hmmm.

Several years ago I had chosen to live in Asheville, a relatively small mountain town in western North Carolina rather than in a beehive like Raleigh. Unfortunately, Asheville kept finding its way onto lists of "best places" in shopping list magazine articles. As long as people kept churning out children, population pressure would continue to rise. Folks simply have to find other hobbies to occupy their time. The inevitable result was that traffic was getting heavier, housing prices kept rising, and the small town I'd moved to had become a small city after all. There was no escaping the encroaching advance of civilization.

Raleigh was a real city, an anthill of activity. Lots of traffic, lots of cars ignoring stop signs and running yellow lights, lots of people jaywalking, lots of rules to break. I don't care for the crowding, the anarchy of a mass population.

But with all its urban problems and a burgeoning population, Raleigh was a fascinating parade to study as it went by. The variety of races and faces, body shapes, clothing styles and attitudes was endless. And every one of these people had a story, one or many, stories from family histories or stories of their very own daily lives. I was a student of it all, a lay anthropologist, if you want to put a label on me. I may be a true curmudgeon and not like people in the aggregate, but I loved the stories, loved the tangled messes people found themselves in, often of their own inadvertent making. That's what made my life interesting after all.

I wandered about the downtown for a while, up this street, down that alley connecting two boulevards, watching my fellow humans at their tasks as they rushed from place to place. Civilization in mid-stride, with only an occasional stumble.

Lunch With a Twist

Without any planning or paying attention to my route, I found myself across the street from *Caffé Luna*. As I looked, who should come strolling by but Himself, Wallace Arrington, attorney-at-law, gun collector, suffering husband, father to a pair of children he could have well done without, and my current temporary employer.

A guy in a suit came rushing up to him, stopping him in his tracks. There was a heated exchange, complete with grimacing and hands waving in the air. There were hot words too, louder than conversation, but not loud enough to make out over the traffic noise. Arrington gestured to calm the man, but the guy wasn't having it. He turned and went off quickly, pissed off about something. Arrington wagged his head back and forth as he watched the man go.

"Wally," I called out.

Arrington peered around with something of the look of a hunted animal, a look I wouldn't have expected from a self-confident middle-aged lawyer like himself. He spotted me across the street and waved me over. Minutes later, we were being seated at a window table by Parker, the restaurateur. He took our drink order and left us.

Arrington lost no time. "I think I'm being followed," he confided. A waiter delivered our drinks, a double bourbon for him, a Drambuie for me.

I leaned forward in my chair, my Drambuie forgotten for the moment. "What are you talking about?"

"I'm being followed. I'm sure of it. I keep seeing the same people out in the street. Well, the same person anyway. A woman."

"Now, why would a woman be following you? You been playing around a little on the side?" I teased.

"No. It's nothing like that. I don't know why anyone would follow me. Maybe someone hired her. Maybe she's a detective or something, like that Kinsey Milhone character."

He glanced out the restaurant window.

"There she is now." He pointed. "Down the street at that outdoor café. The one with the dark hair and the bomber jacket."

The woman was too far away to make out any details, but she looked much like the one I'd met only half an hour ago as I began my wandering. This was a bit too weird. A coincidence? I'm not sure I believe in such things. Something was going on, and we needed to know what it was.

"That looks like the woman I knocked to the pavement when I came out of your house half an hour ago. I'd swear it was the same one. Same jacket, same hair, same jeans."

Arrington rose. "I'm going to find out who she is." He rose, downed his bourbon, and made to move away from the table. I grabbed his arm and pulled him back into his chair.

"Better not. It's no big deal anyway. Just a coincidence."

"Oh, yeah? I've seen her several times around town this morning. And now you tell me she was in front of my house. That's no coincidence, boyo. That's stalking."

I pulled out my cell phone. "I'll call Perez. Let him handle it."

The woman had gotten up from her street-side table and was ambling in our direction though on the other side of the street. As she passed *Caffé Luna* she made a pistol with forefinger and thumb and took an imaginary shot in our direction through the window.

"That does it," barked Arrington, getting up from the table, knocking his chair over in the process. The chair hit a waiter who was passing him with a tray of spaghetti dishes, sending the waiter to the floor and pasta and red sauce all over an older couple at the next table.

"Damn!" Arrington spat as he tried to get free of the mess. As he reached the restaurant's front door, I turned to look out the window. The woman was gone, not to the right, not the left. She was gone. Evaporated. But Wally had made his point, as had the woman with that final pistol gesture. But wait a second. She'd been following him? I'm the one who'd bumped into her outside Arrington's home. Who was her gesture aimed at: Arrington or me? And perhaps more importantly, why?

I sat at the library table, my laptop open in front of me. Perez stalked back and forth peppering me with questions at a hurricane wind speed.

"Can you describe her? You actually talked to her, right? How far away were you?"

"I don't know. I don't know." I threw up my hands in surrender, then transformed them into a "stop" gesture in front of me. "Whoa! Wait minute."

"Why? You remember something?" Perez persisted.

"I think so. Dark hair. She had dark hair."

"How dark? Brown? Black? How long was it? Real long? Or real short?"

"Wait a minute. Give me a break, will ya?" I caught my breath. "Dark brown. It was dark brown. And down to here." I flat-handed a line at my chin. "Straight. And… and she had a deep dimple in her chin. Like Kirk Douglas."

"Like who?"

"He's an actor. Before your time, I guess."

Perez scribbled in his little wire-bound notebook with a pencil stub he'd produced from somewhere. "How do you spell that? D O U…"

"Like the name Douglas. You want a longer pencil? I have pencils over here," I offered, gesturing to my research supplies on the library table.

He held up the inch-long stub with its worn eraser between thumb and forefinger like a trophy.

"You've never seen a pocket pencil before? I thought everyone carried one. You don't?" He turned toward the door as Arrington came into the room. "Hey, Arrington. Show the kid your pocket pencil," he jibed.

Arrington stopped and his brow furrowed. "What are you talking about?"

"Never mind." Perez withdrew his demand. "Just a little joke. Hey, you know anyone named Douglas?"

Arrington ignored the question. "Can you find this woman? The thought of her wandering around town loose is making me crazy. She's dangerous," Arrington asserted.

Perez sighed. "Even if we find her, we can't arrest her. She hasn't done anything."

"Maybe not yet," Arrington added, "but I don't want her around."

"You might could get a restraining order to keep her at a distance," I suggested. "You're a lawyer, remember? You don't know how to do that?"

"But you'd need her name and get her to stand up in front of a judge," Perez added.

"Fat lot of good that would do," Arrington groused. "Suppose she's got sniper training?"

Perez laughed. "You're being paranoid about coincidences. Calm down. Aren't you lawyers supposed to be cold and unfeeling, emotionally flat?"

"Where the clients are concerned, certainly. But I'm the one who's being stalked here. That's different. And besides, twice might be a coincidence, but three times and pointing a finger gun at us? Come on, Perez. She threatened us."

"Y'know…" I meditated aloud. "That woman looked too familiar. I think I might have seen her at the auction house. Before the shooting started."

Perez cocked his head and looked at me with new interest. "Now we're getting somewhere. Are you sure about that? How sure are you? If I can tie her to the shooting… well, we might be able to pick her up as a material witness to a crime, maybe even hold her as a suspect." He rubbed his unshaven chin, producing a rasping sandpaper sound.

Perez stood and dropped his notebook and stub pencil into his suit jacket pocket. "Look, I'll post that we want her for questioning. That might be all I can do. The rest depends on whether we find her or not. And then, if we can hold her at all, we can't hold her very long. There are legal limits." He gave a half shrug and left. No doubt we'd be seeing him again.

And that was that. Arrington would have to deal with his terror on his own. Me? I was curious, curious as hell, but I didn't think it was my problem. I think the woman was out to ruffle Wally. And boy, did she ever!

Alone in the library, Arrington and I stood looking at one another. I shrugged. "How do I always find myself in the middle of other people's issues? It happens on every job I take. It's become the pattern of my life."

"Maybe you're just lucky. My world is similar. People rarely come to an attorney when things are going well. It's always a crisis of one sort or another: the unexpected DUI, a nasty divorce, a contested accident claim, suing a crooked partner who's been embezzling for years. I live on other people's travail. I used to think that I lived a predatory existence because of all that. But to be candid, that feeling didn't last long after the money started to roll in." He shook his head from side to side. "What we become..." he said with a sigh.

So Arrington had a conscience after all, or at least he'd had one when he started out. But with time, it seems he overcame his ethical qualms. The antidote had been cash flow.

Arrington walked to a shelf and pulled down a brass-bound wooden box. It wasn't fancy or so big that it was awkward to handle. It was a bit larger than a shoebox. He placed it on the library table. Fumbling in his pocket, he pulled out a large brass key which he used to unlock the box.

"I probably should have given you this when you arrived, but I didn't even remember having it until this morning. Creeping Alzheimer's?" He chortled. "Anyway, this was passed down the family along with the gun. In fact, this was where I found the gun in the first place, in this very box. I haven't looked in here since I married Celine. That was quite a while ago," he mused.

He swung the top open and pushed the box toward me. "Maybe you'll find something useful in here."

With that, he left the library, perhaps off to solve the monumental problems imagined by his clients, perhaps to find several more double bourbons.

Connections

What was Arrington sharing with me? He'd identified the box as a family heirloom, at least as a historical artifact that had been part of the dowry package when he married Celine those many years ago. Celine and his unappreciative children were frighteningly evident in his daily life, but the box and its unexamined contents had receded into his subconscious, not thought of at all through the years of his increasing professional responsibilities and collapsing family relationships.

We all have similar blanks in our memories. Life interferes with the living of itself, getting in the way of the important stuff, shuffling priorities in unexpected ways, thrusting the insignificant to mountainous heights and hiding the significance of the human relationships that should be in the forefront. Cosmic tidal forces push and pull in great thrusts as mother moon and the myriad stars watch our meaningless scratchings in the dirt without emotion, uncaring. It's like we have no control over ourselves.

I leaned over and looked into the mysterious box.

Dry, discolored and crumbly-looking papers looked back up at me. I slid a clean sheet of modern paper under the top fragile-looking ancient document and lifted it out gingerly. Interesting, but what exactly was it? It had a date: September 20, 1871. The printed header said "COPE'S LINE OF PACKETS." What did that mean? It was back to the Internet for me.

A quick search revealed that an entrepreneur named Thomas P. Cope had established the Cope Line in Philadelphia in 1821 to carry mail back and forth across the Atlantic Ocean. He ran five packet ships between Liverpool and Philadelphia and New York from 1841 until the 1870's. That's when steam ships were beginning to replace packets propelled by wind and sail and required a month for the crossing. Steam put the Cope Line out of business.

I knew that during that period, Philadelphia had been one of the main arrival ports for European immigrants. Sure enough, a bit of further searching in the Cope archives found an arrival record for Armond Davis and his wife Bela on Cope's *S.S. Wyoming* in 1871. Jackpot!

Just for kicks, I typed in another search string. That netted me a painting of the *S.S. Wyoming* under full sail. It wasn't necessary for me to find the ship itself, but having the image was pretty cool. As a geek at heart, I thought so anyway.

I reached into the box again…

…and picked up a copy of a government form, a "Declaration of Intention." This was the form that immigrants were required to swear to in front of a magistrate before applying to become U.S. citizens.

Philadelphia also kept naturalization records online. I searched but found nothing for the Davis couple. Where had they gone after arriving in Philly?

Had I been a smoker, this would have been the perfect time to step out for a smoke to think things through, but I wasn't, so I didn't. Instead, I reached back into the box.

What came out next was one hell of a surprise. I held in my hand the document that had caused the rift in the Davidi family: a handwritten copy of the last will and testament of Alfonso Davidi bound in a blue backing sheet, signed and sealed in lawyer's offices in Basingstoke, Hampshire, England on June 11, 1869. Finding the will was a great surprise, and its contents were revelatory.

Most significant was the reliance on the Old World standby inheritance theory of primogeniture. I might have just found Armond's reason for leaving Merry Olde England. As the direct practical effect of the legal mechanism of primogeniture in his father's will, Armond had essentially been disinherited in fact, if not in specific wording. His twin brother Charles, older perhaps by minutes, maybe even seconds, had received the bulk of their father's estate. The estate included the family match manufacturing business Davis Match Works Ltd: the factory, the offices, the plant and equipment. He also got the family home.

Poor old Armond was out. He must have left the reading of the will with one of the Prélat pistols and little else. To add insult to injury, his older brother Charles Davis got the other gun, the walnut case in which the guns had originally been housed, and all the accompanying duelist's accoutrements such as ramrods, bullet mold, and brass powder flask. It was no wonder that Armond abandoned the country that had been his family's sanctuary. He was pissed off.

This was exactly the sort of thing that made a genealogist's life fun and exciting. Sitting in Arrington's library in Raleigh, North Carolina, I was holding a lawyer's copy of the 1869 document that had changed a family's fortunes and forced a schism between twin brothers.

I've seen again and again that most family battles revolve around the distribution of money or other assets. In my own family, cousins had come to blows over several hundred dollars that had been grandpa's will distribution to one but not the other grandchild. Of course, it was due to the machinations of the wicked step-grandmother who was looking out for her own progeny and not the ones that had come along into grandpa's second marriage with him. I hate to see that sort of thing happen, but it happens far too often to be a random event. Greed and acquisition jealousies are traits that are all too human. And people wonder why I'm cynical about my fellow "higher" primates and our basic nature. Sometimes I'm embarrassed to be a member of species *Homo sapiens*.

Though itching to continue to the bottom of the box, I now had plenty to think about. The clues were piling up. It was enough for the day. In old British navy parlance, the sun was over the yardarm for me.

I left the library to find Simmy and interview her about where the Drambuie was kept.

Friday

Davis Match Works

The Davis family in England was a fine example of the new entrepreneurs who flourished during the Industrial Revolution. They were match manufacturers. No, not people who arranged marriages for hapless folks for a fee. These were people who worshipped the Roman god Vulcan and worked with real fire of heat and flame.

Alfred Davis, nee Alfonso Davidi, had trained as a chemist in Salerno, Italy. After immigrating to England, he had experimented in the recently invented technology of the match. After negotiation with the innovative Swedish match chemist Johan Edvard Lundstrom about manufacturing rights to Lundstom's unique formula and process, Davis was able to establish himself as a safety match maker. Beginning modestly as most new businesses do, the business grew and prospered, eventually supplying most of the safety matches used in England and its colonies. Despite the British distaste for foreigners in their midst, life went well for the Davis clan. After all, it was only Alfred, nee Alfonso Davidi, Davis who'd been a "foreigner."

I checked the Basingstoke business directories for the mid-1800s. Davis Match Works was there, located near what is now the Houndmills Industrial Estate. So was the name of the principal: Alfred Davis. A further look at the city directory for the period gave me a home address. My search continued on to the census.

This work that I've chosen to do is sometimes like an avalanche. Datum after datum, name after date after name after date come pouring out of the computer and the genealogical family

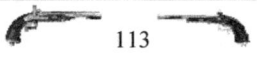

chart builds quickly. At other times, it's like moving a mountain with a teaspoon: a pebble here, a pebble there. One never knew beforehand how a case would go.

So far, the Arrington family had been pretty easy. I had expected the British side to be difficult, mostly because of my inexperience with records on the other side of the Atlantic. As it turned out, the British census would be my road map through the Davis, nee Davidi, line from the mid-1800s up to the present, at least until I reached a census Her Majesty's government hadn't released yet. This is how it went:

The 1861 British census showed a family group at that first Basingstoke address composed of Alfred Davis as head of household, and Charles and Armond Davis as sons. I had father Alfred Davis' will. That had been signed, sealed and dated June, 1870. Alfred had died soon afterward in 1870, so I knew he wouldn't be listed in the 1871 British census, and I'd found Armond and his wife Bela in the 1880 U.S. census.

Sure enough, the 1881 British census showed Charles Davis as head of household and his occupation as manufacturer. His wife Celia was listed as well. A quick look at the Basingstoke business directory for that year proved that Davis Match Works was still a going concern. Cedric Pasqual Davis, their son, had been born in 1868 and was also living in the family digs. By 1891, according to that year's census, both Charles and his wife had died and Cedric was head of household and the owner of Davis Match Works.

Following the Davis history through census sheets and city directories, I was able to piece the family together. To wax biblical, Cedric and Martha begat Neville in 1901, daughter Tara in 1906, and daughter Anatola in 1915. Neither of the girls showed up in the 1921 census. Perhaps they had been victims of the Spanish Flu that took so many in 1917 and 1918.

And so it went down the generations until 1931, the last census before World War II. No census was done in 1941, undoubtedly to keep detailed information on the British population out of Nazi hands.

Neville and his wife Alicia begat daughters Davidina in 1938 and Andromeda in 1956.

That was as far as the easy research went. With two daughters at the end of the chain, if they had married, their lives might be somewhat obscured by name changes.

Backing up, I checked the Basingstoke business directory for 1921. Davis Match Works was still going, but there was no listing for the company in 1932.

What had happened to Davis Match Works? Had the company moved to another town? That's not so easy with a manufacturing plant. Had they gone bust? The match business burned brightly, in the financial sense. Everyone used matches and Davis Match supplied matches across the worldwide empire. If the sun ever set on the British Empire, any citizen with a Davis Match in his pocket could relight it. It was highly doubtful that they had gone out of business.

Something had happened, but what?

Where could I find a history of industrial activity in and around Basingstoke, Hampshire?

I'd start with a search for a book that some enterprising local historian had done. There's usually someone in a town who's obsessive about their home ground and writes the definitive history. Failing a book, a newspaper's morgue is packed full of information, whether reported daily, weekly or monthly. That would be the next inquiry.

I wondered if I could talk Wally into footing the bill for a two or three day trip for me to fly over to Basingstoke to do an on-site search. He already had lots of money tied up in this project. What difference would another few hundred make? I'd ask him about it this evening.

But for now, it was back to the Internet for me, this time to the Basingstoke Library. There was an immediate problem: they didn't have an online catalogue. How could that be in this age of digital everything: remote control refrigerators that reminded one of replenishment needs, stoves that warmed your dinner before you arrived home from work, home thermostats that adjusted themselves to your perfect temperature, remote cameras to watch the babysitter sitting on the children?

I'd finally hit what looked like a fatal block to my research, or at least a significant obstacle to surmount. I say again: a genealogist's life is fraught with danger… well, maybe not exactly danger, but there certainly are difficulties. But that's what I get paid for, so off I went on another tear in a different direction. I'd have to try a more direct search.

A nice feature that the basic Basingstoke city website had was a "Heritage" page. On it, there were several paragraphs giving a short history of the region with its Bronze Age, Stone Age and Iron Age influences. All that had eventually culminated in Calleva Atrebatum, a walled Roman town that evolved to become the nearby city of Silchester. There wasn't much on industry since those days though, and I certainly didn't need to go back to the prehistoric beginnings of the place.

I was looking for specific information about one company that had disappeared from the city directory between 1921 and sometime in the early 1930s. I only had to search the business directories from 1921 forward until the company vanished, then switch over to the newspaper archives to pinpoint the date, and hopefully, the reason.

Aha! I found a significant lead in the form of a pdf: *A Guide to Sources of Information on Basingstoke's History* by Bob and Barbara Applin. That was bound to produce something. Sure enough, it did.

It's a genealogist's joy to find a compendium or bibliography of sources on a topic, a place, or an event. The roads that lead from there can be infinite and the tidbit one seeks might be found after digging into only the first few listed items. That was the case here. The Applins gave me a history of the newspapers that had existed through Basingstoke's life. I now knew what morgues the bodies might be discovered in.

The Great Depression began in the United States in October, 1929, and its effects were felt across the entire world. The English called it The Great Slump, but it amounted to the same thing. England's manufacturing and mining industries were hit particularly hard. The Davis Match Works was no longer listed in the Basingstoke business and city directories in 1931. Was the Great Slump the reason?

I switched to the newspapers and discovered that the Great Slump had nothing to do with the Match Works' demise. Several newspapers for the period just before that fateful 1931 Christmas reported that a fire had destroyed the manufactory along with several other businesses that were located nearby. The general thinking was that those who play with fire long enough will eventually get burned. A match manufactory? With piles of dried wood laying about to make the match sticks and match boxes, unprotected stocks of flammable chemicals, and little in the way of fire-fighting equipment that could gain control over a major conflagration, it had only been a matter of time before a catastrophe occurred.

The fire was a blow to the 96 workers employed at the plant, but it was an even greater slam at the Davis family. Their source of income, power and prestige was gone. The little empire that Charles Davis had built and passed to his progeny was destroyed utterly.

But there was more, both in the newspapers and buried deep in the psyche of the family. Investigators couldn't find a reason for the fire. It was true that fire prevention measures at the factory had been lax, but that was the situation with many businesses that had been established in the industrial boom of the nineteenth century and that laxity had continued on into the twentieth. They didn't have the safety and worker protection laws back then that they do now. Nor were there the sprinkler systems or Halon extinguishers that we have today.

And there was even more. Investigators were told by family members that they suspected the fire had been started on purpose to even an old score. There had been a will years before in 1870 that had caused a rift in the family. The bond between twin brothers had been irretrievably broken by the venerable legal theory of primogenitor that the will had followed. The older twin, perhaps older only by seconds, had inherited the Davis Match Works established by their father, along with his other properties. The younger brother had received little, if anything, and had left for America with his pregnant wife as soon as he could. Had his descendants, still harboring a grudge against the family patriarch, returned to England to destroy the Match Works and set things right in the family accounts?

Their business was ruined, and Tara Davis, a spinster sister who ran the business with her brother Neville, was killed in the blaze. There was little of their former lives to salvage.

Despite thorough professional investigation, no evidence of arson had been discovered, and the case had been classified as an accident and shelved unsolved. No one was blamed by name, no one was charged with a crime, no one was arrested and tried, and no one was punished.

Nonetheless, the family from then on believed the fire had not been an accident. The arson theory, once voiced, became fixed in the minds of the British branch of the Davis clan. It became their mantra, the stated reason for their downfall and their failure to ever recover financially.

The Family Vanishes

After the 1931 fire and the catastrophic disruption it caused, the family disappeared from the various Basingstoke directories. There were other Davis names listed, Davis being a common English name, but Neville and his wife Alicia were gone. Where to? This was the next tracking problem for me to tackle. Where to begin...

Back to the census, of course. I looked for a name index and found there were several dating all the way from 1841 through 1911. That was great as far as it went, but it didn't help me. And there were other problems. I needed indexes that began in 1931. The census records for 1931 had been totally destroyed by fire in 1942, though it had been determined that the fire was not caused by German bombing or sabotage. It had simply been an accident. Fire, the great purifier, the great cleanser, had become my nemesis.

A general search for British census records revealed a few more pertinent and disappointing facts. There was no census done in 1941. The war was going full bore and the strategic decision to not do a census enumeration was made to keep the Germans as ignorant as possible about the British population. The next census done was in 1951. That's where my next search would have to be made. I searched.

No luck. The Census Act of 1920 prohibited disclosure of the census results. The law doesn't say so directly, but a 100 year stricture on release of the census was established in a later document referred to as the "Lord Chancellor's Instrument No. 12 of 1966," which states that census data could not be released until 100 years had passed after the enumeration. If I were still looking for the Davis family in 2052, my luck would change. As of the moment, forget it; I was at a dead end.

Frustrated and not knowing which way to turn next, I decided it was time for a break. Closing my laptop, I stood and stretched. My back popped, low down in the lumbar region, scaring me for a second. I knew I'd been sitting hunched over the keyboard too long. Luckily, the pop wasn't a muscle pull or a dislocation. Instead, I felt a release of tension, a freeing of trapped muscle and tendon. It truly felt like a highly successful chiropractic adjustment. I was ready for action.

I reached into my pocket and pulled out the Obregon-Meller auction house business card. *What the hell,* I thought. *What have you got to lose, Bones? Your dignity? You know there's hardly any of that left. Go for it.*

I punched the number into my cell phone.

"Obregon-Meller. Can I help you," a sweet young female voice answered.

"Is Odile around?"

"Hold, please." There followed a series of barely audible clicks.

"This is Odile. Who is calling, please?"

"It's me, Ben Bones. I was in the other day with Wally Arrington."

"Oh, yes, I remember," she said, her exotic accent painting her words with more depth than the words by themselves might have expressed.

"I'm heading out to lunch and wondered if you were free for an hour or so."

"Oh, Mr. Bones… Let me check my calendar." I heard paper rustle. "We're between auctions just now, and with all the fuss of the past few days… Yes, I can meet you. Half an hour at The Bagelry?"

"I'm not familiar with the town but I can find it. Half an hour then. Great. I'll see you there."

Wow! Odile, here I come.

The Bagelry

I checked myself over quickly to be sure I wasn't the mess I usually am. Living the bachelor life, style wasn't something I worked at. I wore jeans most of the time, along with a polo shirt. My fashion concession was a fancy belt buckle, with a cast brass demon or cloisonné dragonfly. Beyond that, I was dimly aware that other people paid much more attention to themselves and how they presented to the world at large. To me, it seemed like wasted time, money and effort. Who did I have to impress?

Zig, Arrington's chauffeur and bodyguard, was lounging in the hall with a newspaper on his lap when I came down the stairs with Arrington's legal hounds Guilt and Innocence following me. Simmy, who had been talking with him, turned quickly and seemed to flee down the hall toward her kitchen realm.

"Going out? You need a ride somewhere?" Zig asked.

I didn't need to think about it. "Yeah, that would be great. You know where the Bagelry is?"

"Sure. Popular place. Good food there. I eat there myself sometimes."

In no time at all, we were cruising through Raleigh on the way to my sizzling hot lunch date.

Lunch went as expected. I was my usual awkward self. The mere presence of a beautiful woman always unnerved me. I can't say why. I've tried to figure it out, but have never come to any firm conclusion. Maybe there had been an embarrassing incident early in my youth, but it would probably require hypnosis or scopolamine to root it out. The syndrome had surfaced after my wife's murder. I'd learned to live with it.

Odile, the exquisite and personable South or Central American beauty handled the situation like the "people person" she was. She had far better people skills than I would ever need, let alone ever develop. I mean, I work in isolation, don't I? I'm generally tucked away in a library by myself or sitting at home in my underwear and a T-shirt banging away on my laptop.

After ordering our meal, she put me at ease with some basic questioning.

"Mr. Arrington has you doing work for him? I have that right, yes?" she asked in her charming and disarming idiomatic way.

"Yes." I felt flushed. "He's asked me to find a family artifact for him. To do it, I've got to track his family backwards in time, then track the British branch forward again. Right now, my mind is in England around the time of World War II. Frame of reference."

"Interesting work? I mean, it must be if you do that sort of thing for a living. Otherwise, why do it?" she asked coquettishly. Her delicious accent made my work sound far more exotic than it actually was.

"I used to be an accountant," I admitted. "It was terribly boring. But some things happened that changed my plans, my life, and my view of the world."

"Should I ask what happened?"

"I'd prefer not to talk about. It wasn't very pleasant. I'd rather talk about us."

Her eyebrows rose. "Us? What about us?"

"Well…" I didn't know what to say. I'd probably already said too much… and not enough at the same time. "I mean… I thought…"

She laughed at my obvious embarrassment. "Oh, I see."

I was sure she did see. She'd been through this same scenario a few times, I'd bet. A beauty like her, with her own successful business in the capital of the state, was probably under constant onslaught by hopeful suitors.

Our lunch was interrupted by the appearance at our table of none other than Victor Arrington. He was with a young woman. Their noses were exact copies, and looked like Arrington's. The woman was shorter than Victor, and wore a harlequin costume… at least that's what it looked like to me. It was probably the height of local fashion.

"Hi there, Bones. Hi, Odile. Lunch, eh?" Victor was all smiles, a real glad-hander. The woman looked like she was having the worst time of her life. Victor introduced her. "This here's Fiona. Y'know… my sister."

An interesting development. The estranged sister has emerged from Raleigh's theatrical underground.

"Er, nice to meet you," I said rising from my chair and putting my hand out to shake hers. She ignored the hand.

"Don't go to any trouble," she snapped. "This was his idea." She pointed at her brother with a hitchhiker's thumb.

Victor was grinning like a Cheshire cat, obviously enjoying the interplay. He snickered. "Come on, Fee. Let's leave the lovebirds to finish their lunch." He flipped something into the air toward me. I snagged it. It was a small vial of emerald fluid. The label said *Love Potion #10.*

"Here you go, Bones. This oughta help. Down the hatch. It'll give you the courage to act." He laughed out loud as he dragged his sister off by a handful of her colorful sleeve.

"What was that about? Strange people," Odile said.

"Those are Wally Arrington's kids."

"Kids, indeed. They're both nuts. Locos." She tapped the side of her head with a forefinger.

"It runs in the family," I explained. "You should meet the mother. Blood runs true."

Odile cocked her head. "I only know Mr. Arrington. He attends many auctions. He seems nice enough."

"He's a lawyer. How nice could he possibly be? Still, he's hired me to do a job for him, so I should keep my opinions to myself."

She smiled broadly. "I can keep a secret, Ben. My business has a confidential aspect, too. Buyers and sellers sometimes want to keep their business quite private."

I took a chance. "Can I see you again? I'll be in town for a few more…"

"Oh," her lips formed a perfect circle of surprise and her eyes widened. "You're quite charming, for an American that is, but I don't think that would be a good idea, no. We're preparing our next auction and I'm very busy just now. Besides, I'm dating someone. Detective Perez. You know him, yes?"

Great, I thought. *I don't stand a chance against a local Spanish-speaking detective.* "Oh," I echoed. And that was that.

It was a good meal, but it ended as inconclusively as all my expectant dates did: conclusively against my interests. Since the murder of my wife and unborn child so many years ago, I've been consistently unsuccessful with women. Perhaps I don't try hard enough. Maybe it was the fear of losing someone close to me again. Yeah, that was probably it. But there were other obstacles too, like boyfriends, husbands... that sort of thing. It never worked out in my favor.

It was time for me to get back to work anyway. I had plenty to do myself.

Focus, Benjamin, focus.

The Puzzle Takes Shape

Lunch was a bust, but at least I didn't get stuck with the check. Odile insisted that she pay. "After all," she said, "I have a good business and can write off lunch as a business expense."

I was okay with that. Why not? She was right. She had a business with national, and probably international, contacts and customers and was doing just fine financially. I was a struggling genealogist who could barely make the rent every month and got regular warning notices from my internet provider and the phone company. I tried not to rely on my credit cards, but there was always a running balance.

We negotiated a bit and in the end we split the check down the middle. I felt that was the fairest way to handle it. She eventually agreed. I could write it off, too. I was on a job away from home, and every penny I spent worked to defeat the tax man.

Outside, we said our goodbyes. She closed off the event with a gentle hug and a peck on the cheek. Sheesh!

Zig was leaning on Arrington's car across the street, waiting to drive me back to the house. I got into the back seat and sank into a mild sulk.

My life with women was a continuing vexation. I tried, occasionally anyway, catching a date once in a while, a lunch like this one or a movie, but I was no Casanova. Nor an Adonis. And sitting at a desk typing all the time didn't help keep me in shape either. I was falling apart, turning into a dumpling, a potato-shaped homunculus. Yuck! What woman in her right mind would want to have anything to do with me... romantically, that is? I'm a nice enough guy, not particularly hostile, except toward society at large. I never hit anyone, let alone a female of the opposite sex. So why couldn't I connect? I don't get it. And as a result, I don't get none... if you know what I mean. I'm beginning to understand why guys go to hookers and exchange cash for sexual services. It makes more and more sense by the day. Still, the thought of...

By the time we reached Arrington's place my mind was sliding back into genealogist mode. *I'm a pro,* I reminded myself. Professionally, things had been going well. I felt I was close to the end of the search. I knew I could find the elusive British Davis family. It was only a matter of time, and a short time at that.

Back in the library facing my laptop, a simple thought hit me. The factory had been destroyed by the fire in or around 1931. Disaster or not, they had probably still owned the land. I needed to trace that land ownership, to find a deed or indenture document. If the family had title to the land, they might have sold it to get relocation money. Assuming they did, there would be a record of the sale. Sale or mortgage documents might lead me to where they went. It was worth a shot. I now had a trail to follow and dug into the problem, fully focused on genealogy and not my abortive sexual dilemmas, if you'll excuse the expression.

Logging back onto the Internet, I scurried electronically approximately 3,800 miles from Raleigh, North Carolina where I sat to Basingstoke, Hampshire in the United Kingdom. I love the Internet. In the old days, I would have had to find a globe and measure it, then calculate the distance out with a slide rule. How primitive. This was better, faster, and undoubtedly more accurate.

After the disastrous fire that destroyed the Davis Match Works and killed Tara Davis, the remaining members of the Davis family, Neville Davis and his wife Alicia Norwell Davis, gave up on Basingstoke, packed up their remaining goods and moved on to seek better prospects elsewhere. The question was where.

Since the Match Works had been an industrial engine for Basingstoke, the fire and its grim details were big news and had been thoroughly covered in the local newspapers. The hottest reports covered the fire event immediately, then followed the investigation and official proceedings over the course of several weeks. I checked the morgue archives of several of the papers. Perspectives varied due to the reporters' personal biases, or perhaps the political and economic ramifications of the fire and loss of a substantial employer, but the facts were easy enough to find. During the latter part of 1931 and early 1932, the *Basingstoke Illustrated News* in particular covered the story from beginning to the end. That's what I was after.

My work is basically detective work. I'm not looking for a criminal though, just the tracks of people's personal doings and activities, the documentary evidence they leave behind. But it's the same process of finding the miscellaneous facts of people's lives and weaving them into a tapestry that makes historical sense. A genealogist gets lucky by persevering. Just don't quit. The information is… is somewhere. But where? That's the trick: to find the where, after which the facts inevitably surface.

Genealogy is basically a puzzle, but a puzzle with a twist. When you begin a search you might have only one or two pieces. The larger picture is invisible. Each individual piece must be searched for, found, and then added to the mass that you accumulate. Sometimes you hit a major information lode. Most times you don't. It's a little bit here and a little more there. Stand back and look at it all, shuffle the pieces around. You might, I say "might," get lucky, and a picture emerges more clearly from the vagueness.

It took a couple of hours of online button clicking, but eventually I found two articles that mentioned the family leaving the area. One of the articles did even better; it said they were relocating to London. I finally had the lead I needed to track them one more geographical step and closer to the present generation. My search was taking me 50 miles east to London next. It's so easy when you know how.

The Davis family, though their income had disappeared in flames, brought sufficient resources with them to acquire a telephone hookup. Not everyone in London had a phone, but since telephone usage there had begun in the 1800s and was well entrenched by the 1930s, getting a phone hookup wasn't a problem.

London was big on city and phone directories. There were plenty of places for me to look. I felt that this part of my search was going to be straightforward. At least I thought this stage would be as it began. But as the Scottish poet Robert Burns is so often quoted as saying, *The best laid schemes o' mice an' men Gang aft a-gley, An' lea'e us nought but grief an' pain For promis'd joy.*

First off, I couldn't find a listing for Neville Davis. Had he succumbed to the fire somehow after the fact, perhaps from inhalation of smoke laden with his match chemicals? Possible, but doubtful. Maybe he'd gone off to fight the Hun. I punted and looked in military records, inching forward record by record.

It wasn't that difficult to find a Neville Davis in the war records from 1939. Neville, having lost his family's estate and probably in a depressed frame of mind, enlisted in the early part of World War II during the patriotic fervor that swept the country at the time. He entered the army as a private. From what I could gather online, it seems that he never saw actual combat because he was wounded early on in a training incident. This would certainly have depressed him further. He returned to London with a damaged leg. A phone listing showed up in *Boyd's Inhabitants of London* in 1940.

Boyd's Family Unit Sheets were somewhat difficult for me to read in that they were all handwritten, but the information they contained was worth the effort. There were a number of Neville Davis families listed but only one satisfied with a wife named Alicia. I had them nailed. I could feel Arrington's ten grand check bulging in my pocket.

Not so fast, Bones. There's more road to travel. And the road would become rough and uncharted yet again. Genealogy is not for the faint of heart. I have no idea why someone would take it up as a hobby. They'd have to be extremely bored with their humdrum lives, have lost a bet with Uncle Ernie, or were threatened with a lost inheritance if they couldn't prove their heritage absolutely.

No, it wasn't over for me. Not yet.

But having found the correct Neville Davis, I continued through the years in *Boyd's* and other directories, year by tedious year. In 1960, a daughter was listed with the parents. Andromeda Sera Davis had been born in 1959. *What a great name,* I thought. The birth was truly an event of cosmic significance, at least for my search.

Andromeda. A unique name for sure. But I felt there was a danger here.

Andromeda disappeared from the *Boyd's Family Unit* lists as of 1976. What happened to her? Did she marry and suffer a name change? Did she run away from home? Did she die?

In genealogy, one of the biggest problems a researcher faces is when a surname goes missing because a woman marries and takes her new husband's name. I couldn't make any assumptions. I had to have facts. It was back to the newspaper archives for me.

Obituaries produced nothing. The trail, though faint, could still be followed. The nuptial announcements gave me the answer I sought. Andromeda Sera Davis had married one Victor Stefano Amalfi in 1976. I'm not psychically sensitive, but I'd had a feeling. As I suspected, she started using her husband's surname.

I did a general web search and discovered that Victor Amalfi had been a well-known sports figure in England in those days. He played soccer and was considered an up-and-comer. Unfortunately, he'd made the mistake of marrying into a family plagued by bad luck. In a regional championship game in 1978, Amalfi suffered a broken ankle. Several surgeries followed, but the ankle refused to heal properly. That ended his sports career. He was effectively disabled.

But Andromeda carried on. She became a historian and author, which helped me out greatly in staying on her trail. Her specialty area was the mid 1800s, the period of the Industrial Revolution in England. This made her relatively easy to find. She wrote several books on the period. One was especially interesting for me. It was a detailed history of the Davis Match Works and the fiery disaster that ended the family's good years. I found a review of that book. The reviewer panned her as a failed academic, saying that as a direct descendant of the Davis clan, she was too involved to be objective, and her suspicions that the Match Works had been destroyed by arson were mere paranoia.

What? Surprise, surprise. There it was again, that suspicion I'd first encountered in the newspapers that reported the fire when it happened. It seemed that the arson theory had been kept alive in the family over the intervening years. The Davis descendants still held the American branch responsible for the conflagration long ago and the failure to recover in their present.

But whatever people may have in their heads rightly or wrongly, life goes on. In 1983, at the age of 27, Andromeda gave birth to their only child. Carla Davis Amalfi entered the world into a financially challenged family unit with a family legend that blamed others for their situation.

Boyd's continued to be a valuable source for me. Between that and the newspapers, I was able to check on the family at intervals. Carla grew to become something of a celebrity, but in a unique field for a woman of the time. She became a competitive sharpshooter, a skilled marksman in a predominantly male realm. That brought me directly into the present once again. And then came a real shocker.

Carla and her shooting team had been chosen to represent the UK at a competitive shoot in the United States. It was scheduled for the following week. The gun sports publication that I found this announcement in published a detailed article on the team's triumphs and its climb to the top echelons of the shooting sports world. The article had biographies and photos of the team members.

I didn't follow gun stuff. I don't care about that area of human endeavor at all. It was a true anomaly in my life to be on a job searching for a missing historical weapon. I was on a genealogical research job, not a gun job as such. But this Carla Amalfi looked familiar to me. Where could I have possibly seen this young woman?

The article was accompanied by a photo of the team lined up proudly holding their Anschutz competition rifles. They looked like serious competitors with their weapons and shoulder-padded shooting vests, all except for the young woman identified as Carla Davis Amalfi.

Carla Amalfi stood with her arms folded across her chest holding a pistol in one hand, an antique dueling pistol, a pistol that was the exact match for the gun in Arrington's collection down in his basement vault. I had found the missing gun.

And then something else came to me, a revelation that shook me. I had met Carla Amalfi face to face in front of Arrington's. I had seen her on the street and she was the one who finger-gunned Wally at lunch. Had I also seen her in the craziness at Odile's auction house? I wasn't sure about that, but I was certain that I'd been within feet of her on the street.

Perez needed to hear about this.

Revelations

When Arrington returned to the house from his office that evening he was tired and irritable.

I told him all about what I'd found. He was shocked. "You mean to say that woman is my distant cousin by marriage, that she's a Davis?"

I nodded and gave him a thumbs-up. "A fourth cousin, specifically."

"That might explain a lot," he went on. "But why is she after me? What did I ever do to her? I didn't even know she existed." He paused, then brightened. "And she has the other Prélat. That's great, Bones. It looks like you've earned your money."

I was pleased to hear that. Another job well done. I was ready to pack my gear and head back home to my Asheville digs. I missed the quiet of the North Carolina mountains where people rarely took a shot at me or my clients. Raleigh, though the capital of North Carolina, was like a frontier town as far as I was concerned.

"How about if I leave tomorrow?" I said. "I've had enough adventure for a week. I've been here long enough to get the job done and I've got things to do back home."

"Don't you want to stick around until I've made arrangements to buy the gun from her? That was the whole point of all this. The excitement isn't over yet."

I laughed. "That's your excitement, not mine. Besides, what makes you think that she'll sell it to you? She's not too friendly. She finger-shot you at lunch. She might've been the ninja who shot up Odile's place. You might be in danger here. Remember their family legend? They hold the Americans responsible for the economic mess the British family has been in for all these years." I paused for emphasis. "I'd be careful if I were you."

"Aah." He waved off my warning. "Don't be ridiculous. Offer someone enough money and you can get them to do anything you want."

I was surprised to hear that, even from a cynical attorney.

"You really think that? Or are you just trying to convince yourself?"

"You watch," he said. "I'll have that gun by the end of the weekend. Wanna make a little wager on it?"

"I'm not a gambler," I reminded myself at the same time I voiced my position. "But you go ahead. Let me know what happens." I shifted gears. "You want to write me a check for the ten grand?"

It was his deal, on conditions that he defined, but that didn't stop him from giving me a suspicious look like I was trying to rip him off. Was he turning on me?

"Let's call Perez and see what he thinks about the girl," he suggested. "Maybe he can find out when she entered the country. Right now I'm assuming she's here with her shooting team for a competition, but who knows?"

Saturday

Fire in the Night

I've had a few close calls in my life as a genealogist, but this night was one of the closest. It happened in the wee hours, when the world was at rest and all was supposed to be quiet and peaceful. Sometimes though, the least expected random event takes over and runs over our lives.

Did I say random? In fact, it wasn't a random event at all. It was a purposeful act by a vengeful psycho. But that would only be determined much later as investigators dug around in the debris and found evidence of arson. The "who" once discovered would make everything clear.

Arrington's Dobermans Guilt and Innocence were barking all crazy. I checked my phone and saw it was 3:50. It was dark outside, but a flickering orange light came through the window of my assigned bedroom. I thought I smelled smoke. Did I dream that? No, it was real smoke, all right.

Fully awake, I turned on the bedside table lamp, jumped from my bed and pulled my jeans on. What else? Shoes. That would help. I couldn't afford to lose several days worth of work, so I snatched up my laptop and papers, stuffed it all into my briefcase and slung the bag over my shoulder. It was now time to get the hell out of there.

One of the dogs began to howl. The other's bark had escalated, becoming more frenzied. People were yelling. A loud crash sounded somewhere downstairs.

I approached the door and placed my palm on it. It was warm to my touch. Not a good sign.

The bedrooms were all on the second floor. The main hallway, library, dining room and kitchen were all on the first. Maybe the fire had started in the kitchen.

Well, there was no time to worry about that. They'd figure it all out when they searched through the remains.

I cracked the door open and was met by a rush of hot smoke. No good. Couldn't get out by the most obvious route. This was serious. I'd have to be more direct, maybe go out a window.

Sirens sounded in the distance. Rescue was on its way.

Crossing to the window, I looked out. The sirens were louder but my room was at the side of the house. I couldn't see any fire trucks. They wouldn't see me either. I was on my own.

The window was stuck; I couldn't get it to open. I wasn't thinking clearly. It later turned out that I hadn't unlatched it. No matter.

I grabbed the chair from the writing desk, reared back and flung it with all my might through the window. Glass flew outwards, but the chair broke apart and got stuck in the shattered frame. More yelling came from the hallway. Someone was banging on my door.

Peeking out the broken window, I saw that my room was only five feet above a garden shed's metal roof. It was possible to get out. The banging continued. I went back and opened the door. After the initial blast of entering smoke and heat, there stood Zig with Celine Arrington unconscious in his arms. He hustled in, kicked the door closed behind him, and we went to the window.

"You first," he said matter of factly. "I'll hand her down to you." His voice was hoarser than I remembered. He'd been breathing smoke.

I didn't need any further cueing or encouragement. I cleared the spikes of remaining glass out of the frame with the broken chair, hung myself out the window, and dropped onto the shed's roof.

Zig tried to hand the woman down to me, but that tactic didn't work. He was a bodyguard after all, and he exercised and was fit for his work. On the other hand, I was a computer nerd, an out of shape geek wearing a heavy computer bag over one shoulder.

Zig gently let Celine hang out the window, holding her by her wrists. I positioned myself beneath her, arms wide for the catch. He let go and Celine and I landed in a pile on the roof, which creaked ominously. It wasn't built to bear much weight.

I looked up and saw that Zig had disappeared from the window, which was now flowing thick grey smoke. I assumed he'd gone back for someone else.

The shed's roof creaked again. One corner tore loose and curled upwards. We had to get off.

Zig obviously had training and knew what he was doing, so I tried to copy his actions. My arm strength wasn't up to it. I rolled Celine to the edge of the roof, and lying flat and holding her by the wrists, wrestled her over the edge. She fell to the ground, still unconscious. Because I was holding her wrists tightly, I was pulled over, too. We ended up in another pile with me on top this time, but we were out of the building.

A genealogist's life is fraught with danger. Paper cuts? Ha! Burned to a crisp in a client's disaster? More likely on this job.

But why? What was at stake for whom? Someone either wanted something or didn't want someone else to have it. The gun? What was so damn important about an antique pistol anyway? It certainly wasn't worth getting killed for. This whole deal was making less sense as I progressed, but then, they all sound like simple searches at the beginning. Facts may be facts, but situations rapidly become tangled and confused when the humans get involved.

Perez Investigates

We sat outside of Arrington's place on gurneys and stretchers while firemen in bunker gear wandered through the rubble that used to be Arrington's downtown mansion. It was me, a singed Zig, and Celine, who was in an extremely rotten mood. Simmy hadn't been found: neither a body nor any trace of her. She'd disappeared. Of course, that made her a suspicious character to the investigators. If she had nothing to hide or incriminate her, where was she?

Victor? He wasn't around. He rarely spent time at the house anyway except for a free meal or to hustle his lawyer father for a few bucks. And from what I'd heard, his alienated sister Fiona never showed up there at any time.

Perez arrived with blue lights blinking and started asking questions of everyone. Most informative was Zig, the body guard and driver who'd carried Celine out and had then gone back in to see who else needed his help. He was the one and only hero of the situation.

Me? I'm no hero. I'd scrambled out of the house for my life. I understand how vulnerable we mammals are, how easy it is to die by accident as well as old age. Not for me, thank you. I'll persevere for as long as I can, and then I'll put up a fight when the Grim Reaper comes to collect me. He'd better bring a couple of big guys with him to overpower me and drag me off.

"How'd you get this case? I thought you were a crime guy," I asked Perez, curious to know why the only Raleigh detective we'd met was him. Wasn't the force bigger than one guy for a city this size and the capital of the state?

"Oh, they want us to consolidate cases whenever we can. Y'know… if there's any possible link. Here we have Wallace Arrington as a victim in two hostile acts, as well as that threat with the finger gun at lunch. Actually, that makes three times, don't it?" he explained. "Don't misunderstand… I'm the crime guy. The arson guy will be here soon. That's not my specialty. We got a good guy for that. Tony Lumen. Weird name for an arson guy, don't you think? Ever hear of him?"

I shook my head negatively. "I've never been involved in a fire before."

"He's world class. He'll sort it out."

There were more questions for everyone. Anyone suspicious hanging around last night? What time did you go to bed? Do you smoke in bed? What time did the fire start? When did you first smell smoke? How did you get out? What were you doing there in the first place? Why are you suddenly involved in several of my cases?

A disconsolate Arrington sat on the curb across the street with his Dobermans seated on either side of him, an arm around each of them. They had made it out, too. Zig might have had something to do with it on his third trip in. If it hadn't been for the seriousness of the situation, I'd bet that was funny to watch.

"By the way," I slid a zinger into my conversation with Perez, "I know who that woman Arrington and I have been running into is. Digging through the family history I found a picture of her. It's a relative of his from the other side, the British branch. I think she's a bit nuts. Those people think that the American family sent someone back to Merry Olde England in 1931 to burn their factory down. They've held a grudge ever since. This woman is possibly acting to even the score. I'd love to know where she is and what she's up to, what she's gonna to do next."

Perez cocked his head and his right eyebrow slowly rose. "You're sure you can identify her as the woman?" he asked.

"Look at this. I can show you her picture from the Web." I booted my laptop up right there at the back of the ambulance and swiveled it around so he had a better view of the screen. I clicked the mouse pad a couple of times. There she was, her picture clear in the online gun publication's article.

"Very interesting," he said. "You got a name?"

"Oh, yeah. That's easy. Carla Davis Amalfi. Is there any way to find out when she came into the USA? That'll give us a time frame. And get this: I think I know why she's here. She's a crack rifle marksman, a member of that British competition rifle team that's scheduled to compete at an international meet in a few days." I pointed toward the photo on my screen.

"That's interesting, real interesting," he agreed. "Okay, no problemo. It's a simple thing to find out about her entry. I can do that. I'll make a call and have that info by the time I get back to the station. With the threatening behavior and a positive ID, we now have a half decent reason to pick her up."

Arrington crossed the street to where Perez and I were talking, Guilt and Innocence following at his heels.

"Those dogs need to be restrained," Perez said.

"My leashes got burned up, Detective. Besides, don't you have more to worry about than leash law violations? What you gonna do about my house?" Arrington was hotter than the blaze that ruined his home.

"We're on it, Arrington. Don't worry. We'll get it figured out."

"Well, I need to get some stuff out of there, out of the basement where I had my collection," Arrington insisted.

"Your gun collection? How do you know there's anything left of all that?" Perez asked. "By the way, you got any ammunition around here that might cook off?"

"No. I'm a collector, not a shooter. No ammo. And that vault was built to withstand an atomic bomb. I had it built that way special."

Perez changed his approach. "Who would want to do this to you, Arrington? Any recent threats?"

"There's that woman, that Brit. And every client I ever had who hates me for what I charged him or for losing his case. Could be lots of people, though I doubt most of them would do such a thing. A person who uses lawyers generally has a pretty good grasp of the consequences of his acts. People like that try to avoid hassles, not create them."

"Hey, Wally," I interrupted. "Where are we going to stay tonight?"

"What? What are you talking about, Bones? Your job is over," he said hotly.

"I haven't been paid yet. I'm staying at least 'til that happens," I challenged. "Until then, I'm still on the job, so to say."

Perez stood there smiling at my exchange with Arrington. Maybe it was a smirk and not exactly a smile.

"Okay, okay. You can stay with Celine and me when I get us into a hotel."

"My own room, right?"

"Yeah, yeah, your own room." That problem handled, he turned back to Perez. "When can I get into my gun vault? I've got to see how it held up, and there's stuff I need to get out of there."

"It'll be a while. There's still hot embers all over the place. And the arson people aren't here yet. They need to look around before anyone starts messing up the scene. If the fire was set by someone, we've got to find proof of that before anything else happens and evidence is disturbed."

Arrington pointed to the firefighters marching around the ruin tearing things up with their Halligan tools. "Look at what they're doing to your 'evidence.' That's how they do an investigation?"

"Oh, give it a break, Arrington. Just let the process take its natural course. You'll get your stuff... eventually... whatever's left of it," Perez retorted.

That shut Arrington up, at least on that point. He turned back to me. "Come on. I got a text from one of my people. They got us rooms at the Rebel Hotel."

Zig took hold of Celine with what looked like tenderness and the four of us and the two dogs walked to the car and got in. Within an hour, we were ensconced in separate rooms in our hotel with new guest toothbrushes and terry cloth bathrobes. I took a quick shower to get the smell of smoke off me and hopped into bed naked.

Today was for sure an adventure, but tomorrow would be a new day. Besides buying some clothes at Goodwill to replace everything that had been incinerated, what would it hold? Whatever it was, it was bound to be interesting. This job's interest quotient was rising exponentially.

The Challenge

The following morning we went to the hotel café for breakfast. Our party consisted of Arrington, his formerly beautiful but somewhat worn loving wife Celine, Zig sitting next to her, and myself. Breakfast was good because it was hot and needed, but it was standard hotel food, not one of Simmy's gourmet feasts.

And thinking about Simmy, I wondered where she'd disappeared to. What was up with her? The cops wanted to talk with her last night. They probably wanted her even more this morning. The longer she was gone, the more suspicious her behavior became.

Arrington seemed distant, abstracted in some way. Over his third cup of coffee, the one to which he'd had the waiter add a double shot of bourbon, he finally told us what was up.

"I had a weird phone call late last night, before the fire," Arrington began. "I haven't mentioned it to anyone else yet, not even Celine here, but…" He indicated her with an open hand. "Why would I tell her anything? She doesn't care."

Celine sat up straighter and gave him an appraising scowl.

"If I say anything about this, people will think I'm nutsy-cuckoo, that I'm being paranoid," he said.

"Oh?" I said conversationally, my tongue in my metaphorical cheek. "What kinda call was it? A robo-call selling insurance, a plea for a charitable donation, an investment opportunity from a Nigerian prince?"

"No, it was just weird, very weird. It was that young lady, the one you bumped into and who shot at us with her finger yesterday at lunch. The Brit. She called my cell phone."

"She called you? How'd she get your number?" I was intrigued. "What did she want? Do you know her?"…and then conspiratorially as I leaned closer to him… "Have you been playing around?"

"No, but I probably should."

Celine bristled noticeably.

"But, no. It was nothing like that." He paused. "She challenged me."

"What? Like to a game of Scrabble, a foot race?" It suddenly came to me. "Oh, I know. She wants a competition shoot with you."

This was gonna be cool. I knew that she was an expert and he hardly ever shot. He was a collector, a connoisseur of weaponry, not a practitioner of its use. His fighting was done in the courtroom with pointed arguments that drew only blood money. Gun against gun, there'd be no contest. She could easily kill him if that was her intention, call it an accident, and walk away unscathed.

Arrington had gone quiet and had a forlorn aura about him. I waited… a while, intrigued but bored at the same time. It was taking too long to get to the essence of the thing. "So? The point, sir? You gonna tell us about it? What did she want exactly?"

He started to speak. Out it came in a bolus.

"She knew I'd been looking for the pistol. She travels in gun circles, remember? When she heard that someone was looking for the twin to the Prélat pistol she had... that had been passed down through her family… She saw a picture somewhere and knew the gun's provenance. She definitely has the other Prélat and she wants to do a deal."

He pointed a forefinger upward to make sure I saw the point. "But, and here's the kicker: she wants to have an old-fashioned duel, according to *The Code Duello,* the winner to take possession of both pistols, to get the set."

Celine was suddenly more interested. She looked at her husband with bugged-out eyes, her eyebrows, already tweezed into questioning arches, rose even higher on her forehead, up to where they met beads of nervous sweat on their way down her face.

I pondered for a second. "An interesting proposition. But why? I know, or at least strongly suspect, that her motivation is revenge for the arson done to her family's factory back in 1931."

"But there was no arson," Wally protested in a pitiful whine. His face had turned red, whether with anger, or embarrassment, or from the bourbon he'd switched to without the coffee. It was hard to tell.

I went on. "You may know that, and I may know that, and the arson investigators of the time determined that, but once a belief is embedded, it's hard to expunge, especially when it blames someone else for what's really your own bad decisions."

He nodded and agreed in a small voice. "Yeah, I know. I've been around."

"So what are you going to do? You going to the *O.K. Corral* or not?"

"Do I have a choice? *The Code Duello* has been invoked."

"So what?" I insisted. "You're a lawyer, right? Figure out an angle that gets you off the hook. That's your stock in trade, isn't it? Don't you do that for a living for your clients? Besides," I said with an exaggerated shoulder shrug, "this isn't the 19th Century."

"You'll be my second. I'll pay you another grand. How's that?"

"Wally!" Celine interjected. She had been nervously playing with her shrimp and grits, but she'd also been paying close attention to our conversation as it became wackier and wackier.

"No, I won't do it," I said definitively. "Me a second to an illegal duel? Forget it. I'm not going to jail because of someone else's stupidity. That's not my style."

"Five thousand."

"Wally!" Celine interjected again, even more forcefully.

I hesitated. I sure could use the money. "No, I'd better stick to my own guns."

"At least he's sane," Celine spat out as she pointed toward me with an arthritic forefinger. She next pointed at her husband. "You're nuts!"

He laughed, a grim sort of choking sound from somewhere down around his pickled liver.

"How about ten?" he asked me. He was sure of himself and had the money to throw around, so why not ask? If you don't ask the question, nothing will ever happen; if you do ask, who knows? You might get the answer you want.

"I haven't been paid my first ten yet. I did find the gun for you."

"Yeah, I know. And I appreciate that, but don't get snippy with me. I tell you what; I'll give you a bank check on Monday for $20,000. You have my word on it."

"You might not be alive on Monday. She's a competition marksman." I argued. The things we do for money. I tacked. "You got cash?"

"I don't keep that kind of cash around, not at home or the office." Poor old Arrington was getting frustrated with me. "Look, I'll write you a check for 20, you take it now, and cash it Monday morning. That's the best I can do." He spread his arms in supplication.

I was amazed that he would consider her demand seriously. What had happened to the sentence-parsing attorney, to logical legal thinking? Had the professional mind left the building?

"Where would you do it? Have the duel, I mean. It's illegal in every state."

Wait a second! If I'm asking that question it means I'm taking the challenge seriously, too. Am I crazy like the rest of them? I've been hanging around with these folks too long, and it's been less than a week.

"Ahem." It was Celine. "I say go for it. What have you got to lose? That damn pistol?" she tossed into the mix.

Arrington looked at her with ice pick eyes, cold and sharp. "You would say that. That way you wouldn't have to murder me or go through a loud and messy divorce. Yeah. Get someone else to do it for you," he spat.

"I gotta go," Celine said, rising and pushing her chair back so it fell over with a crash. The other restaurant patrons turned to look. "Being here with you makes me sick anyway. Raises my blood pressure. How does it make you feel, dearest?"

Nice, I thought. *The loving wife.*

Arrington, Zig and I watched as Celine abruptly left the café in a carefully orchestrated high-heeled march.

Arrington refocused. "In answer to your question, I've got friends with wild property out in the country. It wouldn't be difficult to find an isolated spot."

"I think you're nuts to even begin to consider this, but it's your decision."

"Bones," he said with enthusiasm, "It's for the guns, the Prélats. That's what this is all about for me."

"But it's not that for her at all," I countered. "It's about revenge, and there's no way you can win this."

Zig slowly and silently nodded in agreement.

An hour or so later, Arrington had a call from the Raleigh fire inspectors. They reported that his basement vault was undamaged as far as they could tell without getting inside it, and that he was free to go collect his stuff.

That finished the discussion off for him. He'd decided to carry the thing through.

Sunday

I'm No Expert, But...

It was Sunday. The Lord's Day for those who are superstitious, those who believe in elves, ghosts, goblins, and old bad-tempered geezers with long beards sitting on clouds tossing thunderbolts down on us with random abandon and probably a good deal of glee.

I don't believe in such things myself. Nor in an afterlife except cohabiting with worms and burying beetles.

But today was a special Sunday. One, two, or perhaps no individual humans would meet their final end at the hands of the other. It was all perfectly illegal, and I was to be directly involved.

Carla Davis Amalfi, representing the British branch of a family that had been ruined by circumstances, blamed the American branch for that ruin. This was an incorrect assumption, but because of a schism that had split the family in 1871 and created bad feelings on both sides, the assumption had become an entrenched obsession down the generations.

The Americans were innocent of the charge, but they had to respond to it nonetheless; Cousin Carla Amalfi had given them no other choice. She had challenged Wally Arrington of the American branch to an old fashioned pistol duel per the *Code Duello*, the winner to take away the family's honor and the matched pair of pistols. She was determined to make the Americans pay. To an outsider's view, it was pretty straight forward. It was to be a fair duel by the *Code* or an unfair murder.

We'd heard from Simmy. She'd called me early that morning. If she was "churchy" at all, she took care of her commitment early, before dawn. I felt she wasn't religious in any traditional sense. She seemed to be an "I'm from Missouri; show me" type, pragmatic and down to earth, with maybe a touch of island voodoo mixed in.

Wallace Arrington, prominent Raleigh attorney and perhaps even a so-called "pillar of the community," was on a suicide mission. That's what I thought. He'd let himself be swept up in a maniac's obsession with revenge for long ago acts that had never been committed in the first place. If I were a fiction writer, I could never have thought of this. The entire affair was too fantastic.

But there we were, preparing for a duel with a pair of antique French dueling pistols. The antagonists were Arrington himself, with ignorant and inexperienced me as his second, standing against one Carla Davis Amalfi, a hot-headed descendant of the British side of the Davis lineage and an expert marksman. She was the one who challenged and set the goals, and Arrington thought he had to respond and adhere as closely as he could to the traditional *Code Duello*. It was a matter of honor, whatever that meant.

In my opinion, it was a dumb thing to do, for either of them. But what did my opinion matter?

Arrington looked a bit ragged. On previous mornings you could see the effect of the liquor on him, but we hadn't been drinking at all the evening before.

"How'd you sleep last night? Are you rested?"

"I didn't sleep well," he admitted. "Rolled around quite a bit. It's not every day I face this sort of thing. The night before a big trial I sleep just fine, but this is different. There's more on the line here, and I don't mean just the gun."

"Well, I don't know what to tell you. I'm not a psychologist, but I can understand the pressure you must be feeling. Remember that's it's not about the guns for her. She's a whack job here on a mission. Just try to relax. You might just get through this."

"Let's go get my damn gun," he said. Zig went to get the car, pulled it to the front of the hotel, and off we went.

We were at the house by 10 that morning. Firefighters were still poking around, but they seemed satisfied that there would be no further flare-up, and they left soon afterwards. There we were, Arrington, Zig, me, a couple of arson cops, and blackened rubble festooned by plastic yellow crime scene tape.

Arrington was after his collection and he pushed Zig toward it like he was herding a bull. With Zig throwing debris aside to clear a path, we found the stairs leading down and made our way to the vault door in what had been the basement but was now open to the blue sky above. The stink of fire and smoke was overpowering.

Standing and looking at the scorched door, Arrington took a key from his pocket and handed it to Zig. "You open it. I can't stand the thought of my collection being burned up."

Zig placed the key in the lock, jiggled it around a few times, then looked helplessly at Wally and shrugged.

"I think the lock got messed up from the heat. I can't turn the key."

"Kick the door," Arrington demanded. "Smack it with something a few times. See if that loosens things up."

I stood and watched, somewhat amused by their interplay, by how the universe and its physics rules interfere with the plans of mere humans.

Zig grabbed an iron bar that lay nearby and started whanging at the door. Blam, blam. The sound echoed in our little alcove. When the metal surrounding the door's lock was starting to become misshapen from the assault, Arrington stopped him. Zig dropped the bar and stuck the key in the lock again. Click. The door swung open smoothly and we entered Arrington's pristine firearms museum. Everything was exactly as he had left it. His vault builders' workmanship had lived up to their hype.

Ignoring all the other weaponry, Arrington went directly to the Prélat's horizontal display case. Producing another key, he opened it. He reached in and with loving hands lifted the pistol from its shaped green velvet pocket.

"I don't even have a way to load it. She's got all the accoutrements," he mumbled, half to himself, half to inform us.

"Then we'll have to wait until later," Zig said. "We'll load them both at the same time and everything will take care of itself. It's more fair that way anyhow." I hadn't suspected that Zig was such a philosopher.

Arrington lovingly placed the pistol into a small padded leather bag he'd brought along and we left, locking the vault door behind us. The rest of the collection would have to wait for another visit. I hoped it would be Wally visiting and not his heirs.

Back in the car and trying to be helpful, I said, "I've done some reading on duels, how they're done, best practices and the like. Wanna hear? It might save your life."

"Sure. Couldn't hurt. Go on."

"First of all, they say to have a party the night before. Not a big blow-out, but something small with friends. Make it a party that'll help you forget the coming confrontation for a few hours. And watch out for drinking too much. You don't want a headache and a shaky hand."

"That's all just common sense," Arrington said. "But that was for last night. This is now. Got anything that'll actually help me?"

"Yeah. I even made a few notes." I pulled out a crumpled piece of hotel stationary and smoothed it out on my knee. "How's this? Stand sideways to your opponent to reduce your target profile."

"Great." He patted his protruding belly. "I don't know how much that tidbit will help."

"Do you have a second weapon, just in case it goes to hand-to-hand?"

"I hadn't thought of that. What's recommended?"

I thought for a second. "How about a switchblade? It can be brought into play quickly and is long enough to hit vital organs. I'm not saying that you'll need it, but it might enhance your general confidence knowing you've got a back-up."

"Sounds good," he agreed. "Zig?"

"Yeah, boss. I'll loan you mine." Zig reached into his boot and pulled out an evil-looking shiny black knife. He pressed a button and a pointy 7-inch blade sprang out of one end.

Arrington's eyes popped. "You ever use this thing?"

"You don't wanna know," Zig said. He pushed the button again and the blade dropped back to hide in the grip. He handed the weapon to Arrington.

"Er… thanks, I think." Arrington slid the knife into his inside jacket pocket.

"Stick it into your belt around back where you can get at it fast if you need it," Zig advised.

Arrington looked at Zig with what seemed like a new level of respect, then moved the knife around to the small of his back.

I went on. "Aim for body mass, not the head. It's a larger target area and you'll stand a better chance of hitting her."

"That makes sense," Arrington agreed. "Say, where'd you get these tips anyway, Bones?"

"That last one is from a cop manual on street fighting. Those guys are trained for this sort of thing."

"Okay, what else?"

"I got this one from a dueling manual from the 18th century. When you aim at your opponent, lean into the shot. You'll not only gain a few inches of distance closer to Carla, but you also reduce your own size as a target."

Arrington nodded.

"You have a black turtleneck?"

Arrington looked at me like I was nuts. "What are you asking me for? All my clothes got burned up. I've got nothing."

"Go buy a black turtleneck on the way there, something with no contrasting design on it and no buttons. Those would only give her an aiming point. You want be a shadow without any features."

"Okay," he said, understanding but getting irritated at my suggestions. "I'll buy it on the way to the duel. Is that all?"

"Look," I told him. "You got yourself into this. I'm just trying to minimize your risk and keep you alive. I've got $20,000 riding on this."

Zig, sitting behind the wheel, laughed out loud.

"Don't start all that again, Bones. You've got my check, right?"

I patted my shirt pocket where the check rested.

"Tell me something, Mr. Lawyer. If a check is signed by a dead person, will the bank honor it? Or does the payee have to wait until probate and make a claim against the estate."

Arrington gave me his most lawyerly answer. "It depends."

"That's what I thought," I retorted. "Don't play the lawyer with me. How about a simple yes or no? I still haven't been paid until the check is cashed, right?"

"Pretty much."

I'm sure my eyes rolled noticeably.

He ignored my challenge and changed topics. "Are we done here? Can we go to the duel? I want to get this over with."

I wasn't quite satisfied but figured that was all the legal advice I was going to get from him. He had other things on his mind, like the possibility of being punctured and killed by one of his expensive antiques.

The Shootout

We drove some 20 minutes out of Raleigh, out to some gently rolling farmland owned by a friend of Arrington's. Zig drove and Arrington rode shotgun. Appropriate seating, eh? I sat dozing in the back seat. Arrington had told his friend that he wanted to go do a bit of shooting, but not what or who the targets were going to be, that he was going to be one of them himself. Zig was quiet the entire trip; he was paying strict attention to traffic laws. We didn't want to be stopped on the way to commit this particular crime wave.

"By the way, what North Carolina or Federal laws are we violating?" I asked to break the brittle silence in the car.

"What? What laws?" Arrington swiveled his head to address me in the back seat. "I don't do much criminal law, but I'll bet there's a mess of them, things like conspiracy, concealed weapons carry, going to a fight with intent to maim or kill, assault by pointing a gun... North Carolina statutes are pretty thorough when it comes to controlling violence and firearms."

"What about dueling?" I asked. "I did a web search through the statutes this morning but couldn't find anything specifically on that."

"Don't worry about it. If they catch us, it might end up being simple homicide and conspiracy to murder charges. No problem there."

Zig pulled the car to the side of the road. He turned and gave Arrington a confrontational stare. "Look, I've gone along with this because I was hired as a bodyguard, but murder? That's not what I signed on for. If I'm picked up with you guys I could go away for a long time. I've got a history."

"Well, you're in it now, Zig. You're my man. You know that. How long you been with me?" He gave Zig a chance to answer, but Zig remained silent. "You gonna stay with me on this or what? I gotta know so I know who I can count on."

Zig considered. "All right. But I'm not getting involved in this here shootout. It's between you and that woman. If one of you goes down, I'm gone. Got it?"

"And I'm going with him," I added.

"No such thing as loyalty any more," Arrington muttered.

We sat there for a second or two letting the import of the conversation sink in. The mood in the car was somber, like we were headed to a funeral. I hoped against reality that we weren't.

"Okay," Arrington finally said. "We all know where we stand. Let's get going."

Zig hit the accelerator and swung smoothly back onto the pavement. He was a cold one, a pro. And me? I'm a genealogist.

The day was clear, a sparkling blue North Carolina sky forming a featureless dome above us. A light breeze ruffled the trees. Birds chirped and insects buzzed by on their various life missions. To all eyes, it was a normal day in the Piedmont.

Carla and her second were waiting for us by a locked cattle gate when we arrived at the dueling ground. Arrington handed his friend's key to Zig. Once the gate was unlocked, both cars drove through, Zig locked the gate behind us, and the little convoy bent on revenge and the ownership of an antique trinket drove into the property on a rutted dirt farm road. The road wound around and up over a small rise that would effectively shield our drama from the paved state road. We stopped and all got out to confront one another.

"Don't say anything to her, Wally. *The Code,* remember?" I teased.

I approached the guy Carla had brought.

"Are you her second?"

He was a big guy, as bulky and impressive as Zig. I thought I recognized him from that shooting team photo in the magazine article. I could tell he was a weight lifter by the lack of a neck. He wore a cross expression.

"Tha's right. I'm Reginald. You 'is?" He didn't wait for an answer. Instead, he reached into the car and brought out a flat walnut box. When he opened it, there was the second Prélat and a bunch of other gizmos I didn't recognize. "Let's load 'em up," he said.

We set about loading the guns, measuring equal powder charges and pouring them down into the barrels. Both pistols were fired at the ground to clear out any cobwebs or other debris.

"You wan' a wad or not?" His accent was pretty heavy and hard for me to understand.

"What? What are you talking about?"

"A wad. Cloth. In the barrel. If it goes into the body it can make a lot of trouble. Infection and like that in 'ere."

A glimmer came to me, something I'd read about that. If the ball passed through but left a piece of cloth behind on the way, the victim could die of gangrene. "I guess not. Safer that way."

"Right," he said and promptly dropped a .38-caliber lead ball into each barrel and rammed the loads home.

We were ready.

"What's yer distance? It don't matter to 'er." He jerked his head at Carla standing quietly next to their vehicle dressed in a black coverall and colorful Scottish tam.

"How about 12 yards?" I asked.

"Wun'erful," said the lifter. "They both shoot at the same time, at the signal."

"And the signal is…" I raised my eyebrows. "How about a dropped handkerchief? When it hits the ground…"

"Right," he said again. "No problem there."

The sky was clear as it had been all day. Little puffy clouds had appeared here and there. The day was getting on. We checked where the sun was and arranged the duel to be side on to it. No one would have an unfair blinding advantage.

We measured out the distance and the combatants took their positions, sideways to one another. We seconds wiped our fingerprints off the two guns and handed them to our "men," reminding them to point them at the ground until the handkerchief fell. Only then were they permitted to raise their weapons and fire. We seconds stepped back and off to the side. We agreed that Reginald, her second, would give the signal.

The air suddenly changed. A cold wind swept across the field raising swirling red dust. It was hard to make out shapes for a few seconds. Everyone got an eyeful. We waited for the dust to settle.

"Ready?" Reginald called out.

"Ready," Carla said in a strong steady voice.

"Ready," wavered Arrington's voice.

Reginald dropped the handkerchief. It fluttered to the ground for about 20 minutes… at least that's how long it seemed.

The combatants raised their arms and there was a tremendous crash, as if the earth had broken in two. They had fired simultaneously.

Arrington fell face forward to the ground. He didn't move. He was dead, shot through the face and into his brain. Blood flowed and pooled around his head.

Carla lowered her pistol, smiled, then slumped into a lump of dying flesh herself. Arrington had followed my advice and shot for her body mass. She'd been hit in the chest. She was dead a moment later.

A crow cawed in a nearby tree. Looking up to the heavens, I spotted three vultures circling high up. How did they know?

Dénouement

How do I get myself into these tangles? All I want is to earn a quiet living online or with my head in a reference book. Other than that, I have no particular axe to grind. Maybe a girlfriend would be nice, though not necessary.

This job was over. Boy, was it over. And there was a pair of bodies to prove it.

Reginald, Zig and I hightailed it out of the friend's property as fast as we could, only stopping to lock the gate behind us. No sense being found on the site of a fresh double homicide. Let the cops figure it out. I watched the news for the discovery of a pair of corpses in a field outside of Raleigh, but there was no public announcement. I have no idea what happened after we scampered away from the dueling ground. I felt bad for the guy who owned the property. He'd have some explaining to do and he had no idea what had happened. And in our rush to leave the scene we'd left the guns on the ground beside the bodies.

Celine? She was probably happy she didn't have to divorce Wally. That would have been a mess altogether.

And what about Arrington's kids? From what I knew of them and their relationship with their father, they couldn't have cared less. Once it was determined that Wally was dead, the three of them would be free and have money to burn.

I was out my promised $20,000. Monday arrived, by which time I was home, and I dutifully went and deposited the Arrington check. I got a call from my bank later that day. "Sorry, sir, but the account that check was drawn on has been closed. No, we have no idea why. No, you can't get the money. There's no money there to get." Banks tend to be rules-oriented. They wouldn't take a chance on being liable for anything, let alone $20,000.

Arrington had been vague about whether a dead man's check was good or not, but it wasn't good if the account had been locked pending probate or closed outright. That was probably Celine's handiwork. She hadn't wasted any time about it. I could use the check for toilet paper.

All I can say at this point is that I've had yet another thrilling life adventure. I learned a lot about human nature, absolute auctions, house fires, antique weapons, the murder statutes of North Carolina, and dueling in general. And I had what was left of the thousand bucks in expense money Wally Arrington, Esq. had given me in his office that first day. Not much to show for a week of effort and witnessing a double homicide.

But for now, I was safely home back in Asheville, waiting for another phone call that would take me who-knows-where for who-knows-what.

I came out of this case unscathed physically, though shaken a bit psychically. As I like to say in jest, "A genealogist's life is fraught with danger." Sometimes people laugh at that. Sometimes they don't know what I'm talking about. This time, it was the flat out truth.

Another job well done. Well, done, anyway. Whew!

Appendices

The Davidi Family Genealogy

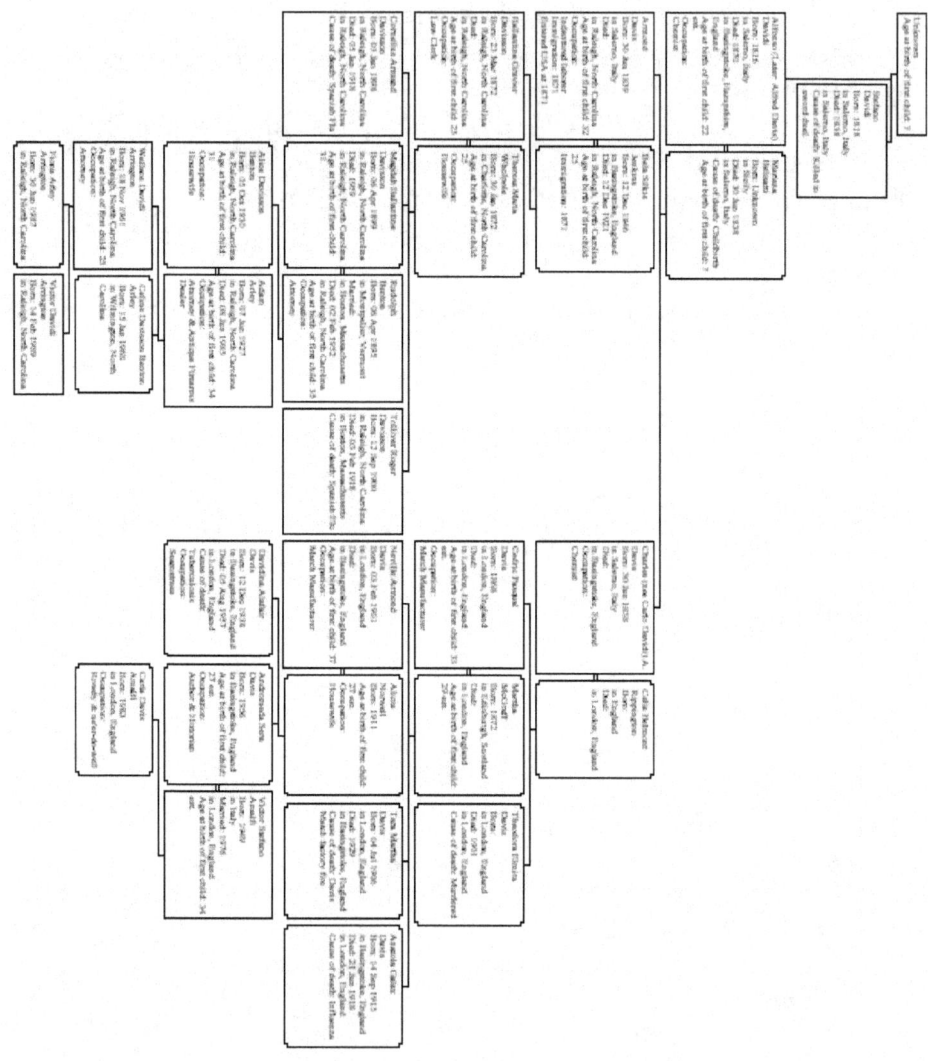

Last Will of Alfred Davis (Nee: Alfonso Davidi)

(This document is reproduced in its original form as discovered by Benjamin S. Bones buried deep in the Basingstoke Historical Archive in the course of his online researches. (The font is 19-point Rage Italic.)

In the Name of God Amen. The Twenty Seventh day of April in the year of our Lord One Thousand eight hundred and seventy, I, Alfred Davis of Hampshire County (Manufacturer), being very Sick and Weak in body but of perfect Mind and Memory, Thanks be given unto God for the Same; and Calling to mind the Mortality of my body and Knowing that it is appointed for all men Once to die, do make and Ordain this my last will and Testament; That is to say Principally and first of all I Give and recommend my Soul into the hands of God that gave it; and for my body I recommend it to the Earth to be buried in a respectful like and decent manner at the discretion of my Executors; I give Devise and dispose of the Same in manner and form following and in the family's Tradition of Primogeniture, That is to say,

In the first place I Give and bequeath to my son Charles the factory known as Davis Match Works, the land on which it stands, all buildings and equipment appurtenant thereto, plus the income from the business, except for the amount of one percent of the net profits to be paid to my son Armond annually.

Second, I Give and bequeath the matched set of Prélat dueling pistols as follows: one pistol, along with its case and appurtenances to my eldest son Charles Davis, and one pistol without appurtenances to my younger son Armond Davis. These pistols are important in the history of our family and are the reason the Davidi family left Italy and established ourselves in England.

Lastly I Constitute and appoint My Eldest Son Charles Davis as my Only & Sole Executor of this my last Will and Testament and I do hereby utterly disallow, Revoke and disannul all and every other former Testaments, Wills, and Legacies, Bequests & Executors by me in any ways before this time named, willed and bequeathed Ratifying & Confirming This and no other to be my last will and Testament In witness whereof I have hereunto set my hand and Seal the day & year above written.

Signed Sealed published pronounced and declared by the Said Alfred Davis as his last will & Testament in the presence of us the subscribers that is to say

Ze. Alfred Davis

John Irwin (his mark)

John Lumbus (his mark)

Recorded in Will Book 13 Page 206, Box 99 Pkg 2428

Proven June 1th, 1869

Recorded August 12, 1869

John Bowie C. C

Code Duello: The Rules of Dueling

Reprinted from *American Duels and Hostile Encounters,* Chilton Books, 1963.

The *Code Duello,* covering the practice of dueling and points of honor, was drawn up and settled at Clonmel Summer Assizes, 1777, by gentlemen-delegates of Tipperary, Galway, Sligo, Mayo and Roscommon, and prescribed for general adoption throughout Ireland. The *Code* was generally also followed in England and on the Continent with some slight variations. In America, the principle rules were followed, although occasionally there were some glaring deviations.

- **Rule 1.** The first offense requires the first apology, though the retort may have been more offensive than the insult. Example: A tells B he is impertinent, etc. B retorts that he lies; yet A must make the first apology because he gave the first offense, and then (after one fire) B may explain away the retort by a subsequent apology.
- **Rule 2.** But if the parties would rather fight on, then after two shots each (but in no case before), B may explain first, and A apologize afterward.
  N.B. The above rules apply to all cases of offenses in retort not of stronger class than the example.
- **Rule 3.** If a doubt exist who gave the first offense, the decision rests with the seconds; if they won't decide, or can't agree, the matter must proceed to two shots, or to a hit, if the challenger require it.
- **Rule 4.** When the lie direct is the first offense, the aggressor must either beg pardon in express terms; exchange two shots previous to apology; or three shots followed up by explanation; or fire on till a severe hit be received by one party or the other.

- **Rule 5.** As a blow is strictly prohibited under any circumstances among gentlemen, no verbal apology can be received for such an insult. The alternatives, therefore -- the offender handing a cane to the injured party, to be used on his own back, at the same time begging pardon; firing on until one or both are disabled; or exchanging three shots, and then asking pardon without proffer of the cane.

  If swords are used, the parties engage until one is well blooded, disabled, or disarmed; or until, after receiving a wound, and blood being drawn, the aggressor begs pardon.

  N.B. A disarm is considered the same as a disable. The disarmer may (strictly) break his adversary's sword; but if it be the challenger who is disarmed, it is considered as ungenerous to do so.

  In the case the challenged be disarmed and refuses to ask pardon or atone, he must not be killed, as formerly; but the challenger may lay his own sword on the aggressor's shoulder, then break the aggressor's sword and say, "I spare your life!" The challenged can never revive the quarrel -- the challenger may.

- **Rule 6.** If A gives B the lie, and B retorts by a blow (being the two greatest offenses), no reconciliation can take place till after two discharges each, or a severe hit; after which B may beg A's pardon humbly for the blow and then A may explain simply for the lie; because a blow is never allowable, and the offense of the lie, therefore, merges in it. (See preceding rules.)

  N.B. Challenges for undivulged causes may be reconciled on the ground, after one shot. An explanation or the slightest hit should be sufficient in such cases, because no personal offense transpired.

- **Rule 7.** But no apology can be received, in any case, after the parties have actually taken ground, without exchange of fires.

- **Rule 8.** In the above case, no challenger is obliged to divulge his cause of challenge (if private) unless required by the challenged so to do before their meeting.

- **Rule 9.** All imputations of cheating at play, races, etc., to be considered equivalent to a blow; but may be reconciled after one shot, on admitting their falsehood and begging pardon publicly.

- **Rule 10.** Any insult to a lady under a gentleman's care or protection to be considered as, by one degree, a greater offense than if given to the gentleman personally, and to be regulated accordingly.

- **Rule 11.** Offenses originating or accruing from the support of ladies' reputations, to be considered as less unjustifiable than any others of the same class, and as admitting of slighter apologies by the aggressor: this to be determined by the circumstances of the case, but always favorable to the lady.

- **Rule 12.** In simple, unpremeditated recontres with the smallsword, or couteau de chasse, the rule is -- first draw, first sheath, unless blood is drawn; then both sheath, and proceed to investigation.
- **Rule 13.** No dumb shooting or firing in the air is admissible in any case. The challenger ought not to have challenged without receiving offense; and the challenged ought, if he gave offense, to have made an apology before he came on the ground; therefore, children's play must be dishonorable on one side or the other, and is accordingly prohibited.
- **Rule 14.** Seconds to be of equal rank in society with the principals they attend, inasmuch as a second may either choose or chance to become a principal, and equality is indispensible.
- **Rule 15.** Challenges are never to be delivered at night, unless the party to be challenged intend leaving the place of offense before morning; for it is desirable to avoid all hot-headed proceedings.
- **Rule 16.** The challenged has the right to choose his own weapon, unless the challenger gives his honor he is no swordsman; after which, however, he can decline any second species of weapon proposed by the challenged.
- **Rule 17.** The challenged chooses his ground; the challenger chooses his distance; the seconds fix the time and terms of firing.
- **Rule 18.** The seconds load in presence of each other, unless they give their mutual honors they have charged smooth and single, which should be held sufficient.
- **Rule 19.** Firing may be regulated -- first by signal; secondly, by word of command; or thirdly, at pleasure -- as may be agreeable to the parties. In the latter case, the parties may fire at their reasonable leisure, but second presents and rests are strictly prohibited.
- **Rule 20.** In all cases a miss-fire is equivalent to a shot, and a snap or non-cock is to be considered as a miss-fire.
- **Rule 21.** Seconds are bound to attempt a reconciliation before the meeting takes place, or after sufficient firing or hits, as specified.
- **Rule 22.** Any wound sufficient to agitate the nerves and necessarily make the hand shake, must end the business for that day.
- **Rule 23.** If the cause of the meeting be of such a nature that no apology or explanation can or will be received, the challenged takes his ground, and calls on the challenger to proceed as he chooses; in such cases, firing at pleasure is the usual practice, but may be varied by agreement.

- **Rule 24.** In slight cases, the second hands his principal but one pistol; but in gross cases, two, holding another case ready charged in reserve.
- **Rule 25.** Where seconds disagree, and resolve to exchange shots themselves, it must be at the same time and at right angles with their principals, thus: If with swords, side by side, with five paces interval. N.B. All matters and doubts not herein mentioned will be explained and cleared up by application to the committee, who meet alternately at Clonmel and Galway, at the quarter sessions, for that purpose.

4, rue des Trois-Frères, Montmarte, Paris, France

    The building at 4, rue des Trois-Frères, Montmarte, Paris, France where Francoise Prelat's gunshop was located in 1838. These shots were captured from Google Earth.

Armond Davis' Packet Ticket

COPE'S LINE OF PACKETS.

LEAVING LIVERPOOL FOR PHILADELPHIA THE TWELFTH DAY OF EVERY MONTH, AND CONSISTING OF THE

SHIPS TONAWANDA, SARANAK, TUSCARORA & WYOMING.

No. 1570   PHILADELPHIA, *9 Month,* 20 1871

RECEIVE in the STEERAGE of either of the above Packets, sailing on or before the 12th of *5 Month,*

may 1871 *Two full passengers*

on presenting this Ticket, provided application be made on or before the eighth of the month,

To W. TAPSCOTT & Co.

ST. GEORGE'S BUILDINGS,

REGENT ROAD,

LIVERPOOL.

Cope Brothers

COPE BROTHERS, PHILADELPHIA.

CERTIFICATES TRANSFERABLE.

Ticket for passage on Cope's Line packet ship found amongst the archived papers of Armond Davis.

Cope's Packet Ship S.S. Wyoming

Thomas P. Cope of Philadelphia established the Cope Line in 1821. The *S.S. Wyoming* was built in 1845 by John Vaughan & Sons of Philadelphia. The Cope line normally ran five packet ships to carry mail between Liverpool and Philadelphia from 1841 until the 1870's. The development of and competition from steam ships ran him out of business.

– *Captured from*
http://www.wyomingtalesandtrails.com/usswyoming2.html.

Declaration of Intention of Armond Davis

Declaration of Intention

Be it Remembered, That on the *6th* day of *December* In the year of our Lord one thousand eight hundred and *71* personally appeared *Armond Davis* before me, Clerk of the Court of Quarter Sessions of the Peace, in and for the said County, who, upon his solemn *oath* did depose and say, that he is a native of *England* now residing in the *County* of Philadelphia, aged *33* years or thereabouts, and that it is *bona fide* his intention to become a Citizen of the United States, and to renounce forever all allegiance and fidelity to any foreign Prince, Potentate, State or Sovereignty whatever, and particularly to the *Queen for Great Britain & Ireland* of whom he is now a subject.

Thomas Doyle *Pro*

Armond Davis

Name Change – Armond Davis to Davisson

COMMONWEALTH OF PENNSYLVANIA
at Philadelphia

At a Probate Court holden at Philadelphia, in and for the County of Philadelphia, on the first Tuesday of August, in the year of our Lord one thousand eight hundred and seventy one,

On the petition of ARMOND DAVIS. In said County, praying that his name may be changed to that of ARMOND DAVISSON, - public notice having been given, according to the Order of the Court, that all persons might appear and show cause, if any they had, why the same should not be granted, - and it appearing that the reason given therefor is sufficient and being satisfactory to the Court, and no objection being made,

It is ordered that his name be changed, as prayed for, to that of ARMOND DAVISSON, which name he shall hereafter bear, and which shall be his legal name; and that he give public notice of said change, by publishing this decree once a week for three successive weeks in the newspaper called The Philadelphia Inquirer, printed in Philadelphia, and make return to this Court under oath that such notice has been given.

GEORGE F. CHOATE,
Judge of Probate Court

Basingstoke, Hampshire, England

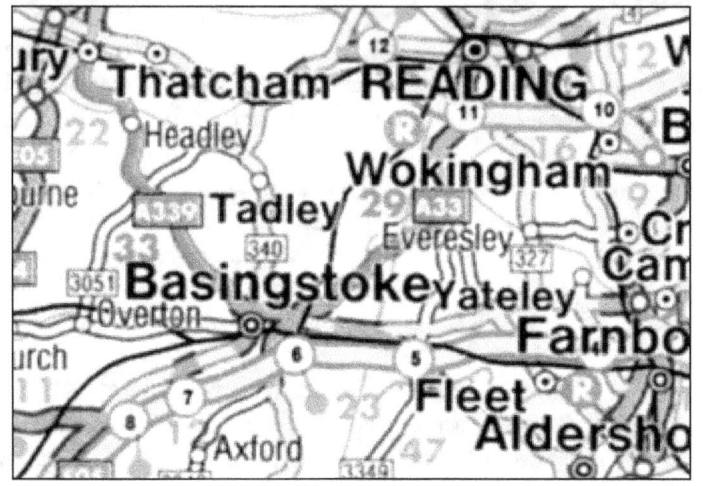

BASINGSTOKE ILLUSTRATED NEWS

DAVIS MATCH WORKS GOES UP IN SMOKE

On an otherwise pleasant October evening, local industry Davis Match Works burned to the ground and the British Empire lost a major match manufacturer. The cause of the fire has not yet been determined by investigators.

Tara Davis, Head Bookkeeper and half owner of The Works, sister of Neville Davis, General Manager and half owner, was killed in the conflagration. No other fatalities have been reported.

Surviving family member Neville Davis suspects the fire was an arson perpetrated by disgruntled American family members. He bases this opinion on a schism that occured in the family when the Match Works' founder, Alfred Davis, passed away and bequeathed the factory to one son and not the other. Investigators have found no evidence of arson, but are determined to examine this possibility.

Weapons

Prélat Dueling Pistol Set

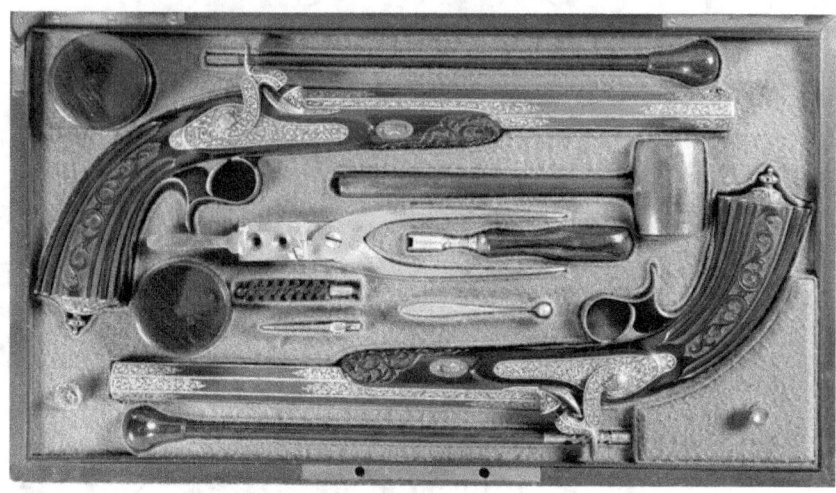

Pair of Cased Exhibition Quality French Prélat Gold Inlaid Percussion Target/Dueling Pistols

Estimated Price: $20,000 - $40,000

.38 Percussion pistols, made circa 1850 with rifled 10-inch octagon barrels dovetail-mounted steel pin front sights and rudimentary rear sights.

The fenced percussion bolsters, hammers and lock plates are completely covered with intricate gold foliate inlays. The elaborate inlays extend to cover the bottom of the trigger guard, the trigger guard finials and fluted buttcap.

The barrels are decorated with intricate, gold, foliate inlays at the muzzle, tang and along the edge of the stock.

The pistols are numbered "1" and "2" in gold on the top barrel flat.

Case contains iron bullet mold, ramrods, and misc other accessories.

Anschutz 1907 Target in 1914 Thumbhole Stock

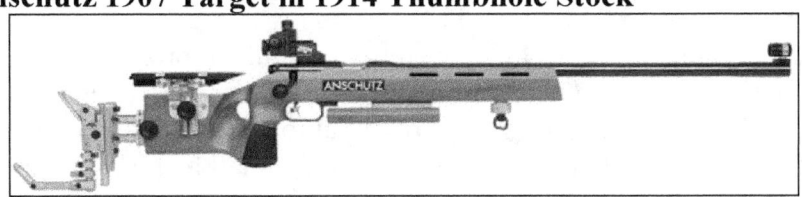

(Information directly from
http://www.anschutznorthamerica.com/match-rifles.html)

MSRP: $3110.00

Caliber: .22lr

System: Single shot 54 Match action, 5018 two-stage trigger, blued barrel and receiver.

Weight: 10 lbs, 8 oz.

Barrel Length: 25.9" Heavy barrel with 11mm front sight dovetail.

Magazine Capacity: NA - Single Shot

Stock Style: Adjustable 1914 thumbhole walnut target stock.

Delivered With: Hand stop 6226, Butt-plate 4765, riser block 4856, MEGA hard case, screwdriver, Allen key, manual with test target

Relevant Statutes

10 U.S. Code § 914 - Art. 114. Dueling

Any person subject to this chapter who fights or promotes, or is concerned in or connives at fighting a duel, or who, having knowledge of a challenge sent or about to be sent, fails to report the facts promptly to the proper authority, shall be punished as a court-martial may direct.

North Carolina General Statutes § 14-17 - Murder in the first and second degree defined.

(a) A murder which shall be perpetrated by means of... poison, lying in wait... or by any other kind of willful, deliberate, and premeditated killing, or which shall be committed in the perpetration or attempted perpetration of... or other felony committed or attempted with the use of a deadly weapon shall be deemed to be murder in the first degree, a Class A felony, and any person who commits such murder shall be punished with death or imprisonment in the State's prison for life without parole as the court shall determine...

(b) A murder other than described in subsection (a) of this section or in G.S. 14-23.2 shall be deemed second degree murder.

(1) The malice necessary to prove second degree murder is based on an inherently dangerous act or omission, done in such a reckless and wanton manner as to manifest a mind utterly without regard for human life and social duty and deliberately bent on mischief.

North Carolina General Statutes § 14-32

Felonious assault with deadly weapon with intent to kill or inflicting serious injury; punishments

(a) Any person who assaults another person with a deadly weapon with intent to kill and inflicts serious injury shall be punished as a Class C felon.

North Carolina General Statutes § 14-34 - Assaulting by pointing gun

If any person shall point any gun or pistol at any person, either in fun or otherwise, whether such gun or pistol be loaded or not loaded, he shall be guilty of a Class A1 misdemeanor.

North Carolina General Statutes § 14-269 - Carrying concealed weapons

(a) It shall be unlawful for any person willfully and intentionally to carry concealed about his person any bowie knife, dirk, dagger, slung shot, loaded cane, metallic knuckles, razor, shurikin, stun gun, or other deadly weapon of like kind, except when the person is on the person's own premises.

North Carolina General Statutes § 14-409.11

"Antique firearm" defined - (a) The term "antique firearm" means any of the following:

(1) Any firearm (including any firearm with a matchlock, flintlock, percussion cap, or similar type of ignition system) manufactured on or before 1898.

(2) Any replica of any firearm described in subdivision (1) of this subsection if the replica is not designed or redesigned for using rimfire or conventional centerfire fixed ammunition.

(3) Any muzzle loading rifle, muzzle loading shotgun, or muzzle loading pistol, which is designed to use black powder substitute, and which cannot use fixed ammunition.

Glossary

Absolute auction – Classical type of auction in which the item goes to the highest bidder.

Anschutz – Maker of world class competition rifles.

Balance – The feel of the weapon in the hand of the duelist: its weight, comfort, and natural aim.

bretteur – A bully.

Call out – To challenge to a duel.

Coming up – Bringing one's pistol to bear on the opponent.

Duel – Individual combat to settle a real or perceived wrong. See *Code Duello* above.

Feel – See: Balance.

Gone out – Went out to fight a duel.

In guardia! Avanti! – Italian for "On guard. Forward!" Command words used to start a duel.

Phillumeny – The collecting of matchboxes, matchbox labels, and matchbook covers.

Prélat, François – French maker of high quality dueling pistols during the early and middle years of the nineteenth century. His manufactory was located at 4, rue des Trois-Frères, Paris, France. Between 1808 and 1812, Prélat invented the first totally contained cartridge. The cartridge contained a fulminate primer, black powder and a round bullet. The contained primer was fired by being struck with a percussion pin This was a great advancement in the orchestration of death by mechanical means.

Primogeniture – A traditional system of inheritance wherein the firstborn or oldest male child inherits the estate of the deceased, regardless of other surviving brothers or sisters.

Second – Operative who does all the negotiating and officiating on behalf of a principal in a duel.

References - Books

Akehurst, Richard, *The World of Guns*. New York, NY: Hanlyn, 1972.

Bob and Barbara Applin, *A Guide to Sources of Information on Basingstoke's History*.

Atkinson, John A., *The British Dueling Pistol*. Bloomfield, Canada: Museum Restoration Service, 1978.

Baldick, Robert, *The Duel*. New York, NY: Barnes & Noble Books, 1965.

Hamilton, Joseph, *The Dueling Handbook*. Mineola, NY: Dover Publications, Inc., 1829, 2007.

Holland, Barbara, *Gentlemen's Blood*. New York, NY: Bloomsbury Publishing, 2003.

Hopton, Richard, *Pistols at Dawn: A History of Dueling*. London: Piatkus, Little, Brown Book Co., 2007.

Kane, Harnett T., *Gentlemen, Swords and Pistols*. New York, NY: William Morrow & Co., 1951.

Sapp, Rick, *The Gun Digest Book of Firearms Fakes and Reproductions*. Iola, WI: Gun Digest Books, 2008, ISBN 978-0-89689-679-6.

Serven, James E. (Ed.), *The Collecting of Guns*. New York, NY: Bonanza Books, The Stackpole Company, 1964.

Traister, John, *How to Buy and Sell Used Guns*. Accokeek, MD: Stoeger Publishing Company, 2003.

Wilkinson, Frederick, *Antique Firearms*. Garden City, NY: Doubleday & Co., 1969.

Online Sources

1965 Raleigh City Directory
https://library.digitalnc.org/cdm/search/searchterm/Raleigh

History of Basingstoke, Hampshire, UK
https://www.basingstoke.gov.uk/heritage

GOV.UK Find a Will Service
https://probatesearch.service.gov.uk/Calendar?surname=Davis&yearOfDeath=1870

Hampshire Record Office –Hampshire Archives and Local Studies
http://www3.hants.gov.uk/archives

Ships named *S.S. Wyoming*
http://www.wyomingtalesandtrails.com/usswyoming2.html

The National Archives (UK)
http://www.nationalarchives.gov.uk/palaeography/

Wake County, NC directories
http://ncgenweb.us/nc/wake/directories/

US Census
https://1940census.archives.gov

GENUKI – UK & Ireland Genealogy
http://www.genuki.org.uk/big/eng/HAM

Thank you for reading this Ben Bones misadventure.
Be sure to enjoy the rest of the series.

Ben Bones and the Deadly Descendants

Ben Bones and the Search for Paneta's Crown

Ben Bones and the Galleon of Gold

Ben Bones and the Conventional Murders

Ben Bones and the Uncivil War

Ben Bones and the Twin Pistols

And don't forget these other books by Michael Havelin:

The Extra Body	*Holy Heists*
Palaver's Hands	*Bloody-Minded Fictions*
The Embezzler Didn't	

And for the kids:

The Loud Library